A KING IN LOVE

Zita was suddenly aware that somebody, a man, was moving between the trunks of the trees, catching only a glimpse as he passed behind first one, then another. She thought that it would be a bore if she had to stop and talk as was customary in that part of the world.

Then as she stood hesitating, wondering whether if she turned her back the stranger would pass by and not stop to chatter, he emerged from between the trees and she thought for a moment he was just part of her imagination.

Then when he came nearer she saw incredibly, unbelievably, that it was the King! He came towards her with a smile on his lips. Impulsively, eagerly, and without thought, she reacted to the feelings that already possessed her heart.

As she ran to him his arms went round her, then his lips came down on hers. All she was conscious of was that the sunset was part of him, the light of it blinding, and his kiss was what she had wanted, longed for, dreamt of. . . .

A

King in Love

Barbara Cartland

A King in Love

First Published in United States 1982
© 1982 Barbara Cartland
This Edition Published by **Book Essentials South** 1999
Distributed by **BMI**, Ivyland, PA 18974
PRINTED IN THE UNITED STATES OF AMERICA
ISBN 1-57723-430-8

AUTHOR'S NOTE

Morganatic marriages in Royal Families were often very successful. His Highness Prince Alexander of Hesse eloped in 1851 with Julie Countess Van Hanke, a girl who was not even noble. She was made Her Serene Highness Princess of Battenburg and was the founder of the great and glorious Royal Family of Battenburg—Mountbatten.

In 1847 Prince George, Duke of Cambridge, a cousin of Queen Victoria, married Louisa Fairbrother, a graceful dancer, and was very happy with her.

His Majesty King Alexander of Greece secretly married Aspasia Manos, the daughter of his father's Aide-de-Camp. She was given no rank or title, but their daughter became Her Royal Highness Princess Alexandra of Greece.

Chapter One
1865

HIS Majesty King Maximilian rose from the couch on which he had been lying and put down his glass.

"I must go back," he said.

"Mais non, mon Brave!"

The cry came from the red lips of the woman looking at her reflection in the mirror.

She was regarding not her face, which was very attractive, but the necklace of large rubies set in diamonds which encircled her white throat.

"You cannot leave so quickly," she said.

Her fascinating accent transformed her slightly common voice into something very alluring.

Then as if she thought the protest was not enough, she moved towards the King, letting her negligé of chiffon and lace fall open as she did so.

"Do you think your present becomes me, *mon cher?*" she demanded, standing in front of him.

His eyes were not on the necklace but on the exquisite figure below it, which had already enraptured Paris.

La Belle, for that was the name by which she was known on the stage, smiled knowingly, and very slowly with the merest movement of her shoulders let her negligé fall to the floor at her bare feet.

Her skin was very white, her waist tiny, and her breasts and hips curved in a manner which was decreed by fashion but was seen in such perfection on very few women.

1

She stood dramatically still, watching the King's eyes roam over her body.

Then with an inarticulate little sound she moved towards him, folding her arms round his neck, her lips seeking his. . . .

*

A long time later the King walked to the mirror to tie his cravat.

They had now exchanged places and *La Belle* was lying on the couch in an attitude of satisfied exhaustion, while the ruby necklace still gleamed against her white skin.

"You have made me late," the King said, "but doubtless the Prime Minister will accept my explanation that I was engaged on important business."

"What could be more important than me?" *La Belle* enquired.

"The Prime Minister could find quite a number of answers to that!" the King replied with a smile.

Having finished tieing his cravat, he looked at the reflection of his own face mockingly, almost as if he enjoyed the cynical lines etched from nose to mouth.

Watching him, *La Belle* thought that even were he not a King she would have found him the most ardent and satisfying lover she had ever known, and she could speak from long experience.

Seduced at the age of twelve, she had climbed to stardom by a succession of beds until she appeared in *Le Théâtre Impérial de Châtelet,* where the King had seen her.

Her lovers had included Dukes, Marquises, and a somewhat obscure Italian Prince, but a King had a glamour that she found irresistible.

The fact that he was also wealthy and was prepared to make life very comfortable for her was enough to persuade her to leave Paris and come with him to Valdastien, the country over which he reigned.

There was a private Theatre at the Palace where she could dance whenever she pleased to a distinguished audience.

But she found it more exciting to dance alone for the King in the *Château* where he had installed her, which had been built a century earlier in the gardens of the Palace.

It was the King's grandfather who had first housed a mistress there when he was too old to travel to the Capital to enjoy the pleasures that only a beautiful woman could give him.

To facilitate the arrangement even further, the *Château* was connected to the Palace by means of an underground passage which could be entered from the Royal Study through a secret door to which only the Monarch held the key.

"When will you come again?" *La Belle* asked.

She listened intently for his answer, never being quite certain what he would reply.

Even as she waited she knew it was foolish to try to tie the King down to a time or even a particular day when he would visit her again.

Omnipotent, a law unto himself, he valued his independence above everything else, and she knew that if she had been wise she would have said nothing, but merely waited impatiently as she had done before until he condescended to visit her.

In all her previous love-affairs she had so dominated the men who desired her that she kept them on their knees and could either lift them to ecstasy or spurn them into a despond of despair.

The King, however, was different.

Although she knew she excited him and he certainly rewarded her for the enjoyment she gave him, she was never quite sure if tomorrow she would not find herself travelling back to Paris without being given any explanation of her dismissal.

As he turned from the mirror she rose from the couch, pulling the soft folds of her negligé round her again, knowing with the wisdom of her trade that it was only foolish women who were abandoned when a man no longer desired them.

She stood appraising him with her dark eyes slanting a little as he shrugged himself into his tight-fitting coat, which revealed his broad shoulders and the athletic strength of his figure.

Then she said softly:

"You are very handsome, and when you leave me I shall be counting the hours until I can tell you once again how violently my heart throbs for you."

She spoke dramatically, but the King's lips twisted a little as he recognised the lines from the Show in which she had little to say, but which was a success due almost entirely to her dancing.

It was her dancing as well as her superb figure that had attracted him in the first place, and when he was with *La Belle* he had often thought that, as with many other women, the less she said the more alluring he found her.

His eyes flickered over her before he spoke. Then he said as he moved towards the door:

"I might arrange a performance at the Theatre next Saturday evening. I will think about it, and if it is possible I will let you know in time for you to arrange a new dance I have not seen before."

Before *La Belle* could reply, he went from the room, shutting the door and walking without hurry down the staircase towards the entrance to the secret passage, which was situated at the back of the Hall.

When she was alone *La Belle* flung herself petulantly down on the couch, drumming with her long, thin fingers on the curved frame.

She knew quite well why the King had suggested a dance that he had not previously seen.

It was because she would have to rehearse it and plan a new costume and thus would be kept fully occupied during the time he had no need of her.

It infuriated her that her hours should be planned by him, while she had not the power to draw him magnetically to her so that he could think of nothing else.

She was well aware, for there had been plenty of people to tell her, that she was not the first woman who had tried to capture him completely and had failed.

There was a long line of beautiful mistresses who had come to Valdastien and left, if not in tears, certainly with their egos deflated and forced to realise that they were not as irresistibly attractive as they had believed themselves to be.

"You will find the King generous, considerate, and delightfully passionate," one of her friends had told *La Belle* before she left Paris, "but he is also elusive, indifferent to female suffering, and invariably and infuriatingly out-of-reach."

La Belle had not believed her, being quite certain that even if the whole world of women had failed to capture the heart of Maximilian, she would succeed.

Now she knew that while he loaded her with jewels, while he aroused her desire as she was able to arouse his, he was still completely and absolutely his own master.

She had the uncomfortable feeling that if she died tomorrow, he would order flowers for her grave, then never think of her again.

She walked to the window, swearing beneath her breath in the argot of the gutter.

She looked out, but she did not see the beauty of the towering pine-covered mountains or beneath them the green valley with a silver river running like a ribbon through the meadowlands bright with flowers.

Instead she saw the Boulevards filled with people, the gas-lamps gleaming above the Cafés, and the audience pil-

ing into the Theatre ready to applaud noisily and wildly as
she finished her dance.

"I am a fool!" she said to herself. "Why do I not go back
and leave him?"

Because the answer frightened her, she turned petulantly away from the window to look again in the mirror at
the rubies round her neck.

She was afraid—like so many other foolish women before her—of losing her heart to a man to whom she was
only a beautiful body and a sublime dancer.

*

The King, having walked along the passage which was
thickly carpeted and decorated with fine walnut panelling
from the forests of Valdastien, opened with a gold key the
door at the end which led into his Study.

As he locked it behind him his thoughts were not on *La
Belle* as she would have wished, but on his Prime Minister,
who he was aware would be waiting for him impatiently.

He was over an hour late for the appointment made
earlier in the day.

However, he had no intention of apologising, for the
simple reason that he believed that he ruled by the divine
right of Kings, and in accordance his subjects from the
Prime Minister downwards must accept him as he was
without complaint.

He passed from his Study into the enormous Baroque
Hall which was one of the finest in the country and famed
throughout Europe.

The Palace had been rebuilt and added to through the
centuries and there was little left of the original building
erected in the Sixteenth Century.

Each Monarch had striven to make it more impressive
than the last, and other Rulers when they came for the first
time to Valdastien were filled with envy at the beauty of the
Palace and the treasures it contained.

The King climbed a magnificent gilt and ivory staircase to the Ante-Room where he knew the Prime Minister would be waiting.

It had always been traditional that the King received his Ministers there.

As if to make them realise they were only a small part of history, the walls were covered with tapestries depicting victories won by previous Rulers, and the painted ceiling was the finest work of a local craftsman inspired by Italian Masters.

As the King entered the Ante-Room expecting to find not only the Prime Minister but at least a dozen of the Cabinet waiting for him, he was surprised to see that there were only two men standing at the window in the sunlight, but not in fact looking at the view.

They were talking in such an earnest manner to each other that for the moment they were not aware of the King's presence.

Two flunkeys in powdered wigs had opened the door for him, and he had the impression, although he could not hear what they said, that they were speaking gravely and almost apprehensively.

The King had, when he wished to use it, an astute perception about other people, and he knew, almost as if a bell rang a warning in his ears, that the Prime Minister's urgent request to see him was not a courtesy visit but entailed something really important.

He advanced towards the two men and instantly they stiffened to attention until as he grew nearer they bowed their heads from the neck in the prescribed manner which was now customary in all the Royal Courts of Europe.

"Good-afternoon," the King said to the Prime Minister.

"Good-afternoon, Your Majesty. It is very gracious of you to receive the Chancellor and me at such short notice."

The King nodded to the Chancellor, Count Holé, who was a man he did not particularly like, and the Prime Minister continued:

"We have something to discuss with Your Majesty and can only hope, Sire, that you will most graciously listen to us without prejudice."

The King raised his eye-brows. Then he said:

"I think this room is somewhat large for an intimate conversation, so I suggest we repair next door, where we shall certainly be more comfortable."

"I welcome that suggestion, Your Majesty," the Prime Minister replied.

The King led the way back through the door and entered into a small room exquisitely decorated with French furniture.

Very much at his ease as he settled himself in a high-backed armchair on which the Royal Coat-of-Arms was embroidered in silk and gold thread, he indicated with a gesture of his hand that the Prime Minister and the Chancellor were to sit down.

They selected two chairs near to his, with the obvious intention that they would not have to raise their voices when they spoke.

The King looked from one to the other of his Statesmen before he said:

"Well, gentlemen? You are making me curious as to what is the momentous problem you have brought me, and which for some reason I cannot yet ascertain does not require the presence of the whole Cabinet."

The Prime Minister appeared to draw in his breath.

"The Chancellor and I were anxious, Your Majesty, to speak to you before the problem, as Your Majesty rightly calls it, is brought to the attention of other members of the Cabinet and eventually of Parliament."

He paused, looked at the Chancellor as if for confirmation, then continued:

"Shall I be frank, Your Majesty, and tell you at once, Sire, what we have come to say?"

"I should certainly prefer to hear immediately what you have to communicate," the King replied. "As you are well aware, Prime Minister, I dislike long-winded dissertations, which are usually quite unnecessary."

"Very well, Your Majesty," the Prime Minister acquiesced. "It is the opinion of a number of my colleagues, which is shared in the country itself, that the continuity of the Royal Line should be assured, for it would be a mistake to encourage certain nations on our borders to think that if anything should happen to Your Majesty, they might have a say in the affairs of Valdastien."

As the Prime Minister had begun to speak, the King had stiffened, and now his voice was quite expressionless, although his eyes were hard, as he said:

"What you are implying, Prime Minister, is that you wish me to marry."

"As Your Majesty asked me to be frank, Sire, the answer is 'yes'!"

"I am still a comparatively young man."

"Of course, Your Majesty. At the same time, you have no brothers, and without a son the line to which you belong comes to an end."

The King was silent, knowing that this was true, and, as if he was afraid he had incurred the Monarch's anger, the Prime Minister went on:

"The people in the south of our country have been very perturbed at the attempt on the life of King Gustav, which took place three weeks ago. As Your Majesty is aware, the King escaped death by a chance in a million, but there is nothing to ensure that an assassin will not strike again."

"What you are saying," the King said contemptuously, "is that there are anarchists everywhere. They were talking about that in Paris when I was last there, and I heard there had even been an attempt on Queen Victoria's life in England."

"That is true, Your Majesty, and here in Valdastien they are not only afraid of an anarchist with some aberration of the brain striking at you, but they know also that Your Majesty is often in danger in other ways."

The King knew that the Prime Minister was speaking of his hobbies.

He enjoyed mountain-climbing and prided himself that at thirty-five he could still climb the mountains with the strength and fortitude he had shown ten or fifteen years ago.

He also enjoyed breaking in the wild horses that were a specialty of Valdastien.

They were captured in isolated districts of forests and mountains, and when the best of them were brought to the King's stable he prided himself in riding those of which his grooms were afraid.

These were just two of his activities which perturbed the Prime Minister.

But the King, with a cynical smile, knew there was another subject on which the Prime Minister would remain silent, although it was in his mind.

When he was last in Paris he had been challenged to a duel by an irate French aristocrat who swore he had seduced his wife.

The fact that she had required no enticement and it was far from being a case of seduction did not prevent the King from accepting the challenge.

Although the aristocrat was a noted duellist who had actually killed two men, he had fallen wounded from the King's bullet, while the King himself received the merest graze on his arm.

All Valdastien had been agog with rumour and speculation when the news broke.

The King was well aware that to the Prime Minister and his colleagues this was another urgent reason for them to persuade him to beget an heir.

"I do not need to tell Your Majesty," the Chancellor was saying, "how happy the country has been under your wise rule and how they look forward to many contented years of continuing prosperity, but at the same time . . ."

His eyes met the King's and he stopped speaking.

It was almost as if he was afraid to say any more, but waited to receive a response that in its violence might almost be physical.

Then as the King tightened his lips as if he proposed to tell the Prime Minister, the Chancellor, and everyone else that they could go to the Devil before he would marry, he remembered that there was a far greater menace to Valdastien.

In Paris last year the Emperor had told him bluntly that he feared the ambitions of Prussia and that he was certain Bismarck was determined to unite all the smaller German states into an overwhelming Imperial Germany which would swallow them up, one by one.

The King, who had never thought a great deal of the intelligence of Napoleon III, had not listened.

Now the warnings, some voiced by other Frenchmen, others conveyed to him in letters from Monarchs reigning over other small countries like his own, seemed to swell up like a tidal wave.

He could see in his mind's eye Germany rolling over the map of Europe, swallowing the small Principalities one by one until they formed a Federation which could face Britain and France on equal terms.

To the Prime Minister's surprise, the King now said in a very different tone from what he had expected:

"I will certainly consider your proposition, Prime Minister. I realise that what you are suggesting is common sense, and although I have no wish to be married or to share my throne, I can understand my country's desire for an heir."

The Prime Minister drew a deep breath of relief which seemed to come from the very depths of his body.

"I can only thank Your Majesty for your most gracious understanding," he said in a low voice.

"I will give it my consideration," the King said, "and I think I would be wise to call first on the neighbouring countries on our borders with whom we could join to form a firm defensive alliance, should the necessity arise."

The Prime Minister, who was a shrewd man, realised exactly what the King was saying.

He too was afraid of Germany and the ambitions of Bismarck, who as all Europe knew was manipulating the weak King William, who was more concerned with his own personal health than his country's greatness.

The King rose to his feet.

"Thank you, gentlemen, for calling on me," he said. "I will notify you of my plans as soon as I have had time to make them."

Elated with the success of their visit, the Prime Minister and the Chancellor withdrew.

When he was alone, the King sat down in the armchair to stare with unseeing eyes at an exquisite painting by Fragonard on the opposite wall.

He did not see the graceful figure in a romantic garden or the cupids which hovered in the sky above her.

He saw only the incredible boredom of having to endure the companionship of a Queen whose only asset as far as he was concerned would be her Royal blood.

He thought of the dreary, pompous little Courts he had encountered in the past on his journeys round Europe and the Monarchs he had met when either a Coronation or a Funeral of one of them obliged him to be present.

They were all very much the same, very conscious of their own importance, terrified of being deposed, and having nothing to talk about but family affairs and the gossip which emanated from other Courts exactly like their own.

Remembering the indifferent food they invariably served, which the King detested, the uncomfortable beds, and long-drawn-out State Ceremonies, he knew that a Queen would bring into his own Palace all such causes of irritation which he had avoided as much as possible.

At the moment, because he was a bachelor, he was able to

keep Court Ceremony down to a minimum and could enjoy himself almost as freely as if he were an English gentleman living on his Estate in the country.

He went hunting and shooting when he wished, entertained only those whose company he enjoyed, and left all the pomposity, except for one or two State occasions a year, to his Prime Minister and other members of the Government.

Thinking it over, he supposed that the people of Valdastien saw less of their Monarch than did the people of any other country in Europe, and because of it, the King thought mockingly, they were much more contented.

A Queen would change all that!

She would expect to appear on innumerable public occasions, she would want to inspect Hospitals, receive bouquets, and drive whenever possible in State with crowds cheering her.

She would also interfere with the running of the Palace, which the King considered was quite perfect as it was, because he had a gift for organisation.

Instead of dining either with his particular cronies or enjoying an evening by himself, reading in his Study or going down the secret passage to visit *La Belle* or whoever else was occupying the *Château* at that moment, he would have to make desultory conversation with some plain *Frau*.

Her Ladies-in-Waiting would doubtless be plainer and duller than she was, and the boredom of it all was unthinkable.

But the King was well aware that he had little or no alternative.

He knew the Prime Minister would not have spoken to him unless he had been seriously pressed by other Statesmen and certainly by the citizens to preserve them from the German menace.

Worse still was the prospect of finding a foreign Ruler to occupy the throne should he die without an heir.

He was aware how the Greeks had searched desperately to find a Monarch to rule over them and had recently elected the second son of the King of Denmark to be King George I.

However, he knew that if that happened here, Valdastien was too small a country to survive, and he told himself somewhat wryly that it was only fair that he should make some sacrifice.

He had been reigning for eight years and had enjoyed every moment of it.

He had been unconventional, but no-one had protested; he had been completely selfish in his interests, and the people had admired him for it.

Now, just as every bill had to be paid sooner or later, he had to pay the price for the freedom he had enjoyed, but he considered it a very high one.

"God knows where I can find a woman I could even tolerate as my wife!" he said beneath his breath.

Almost as if the Devil were taunting him he saw a procession of Princesses pass before his eyes—tall, short, fat, thin, dark, fair, red-headed, they all in the King's eyes looked exceedingly unattractive and the idea of touching one of them made him shudder.

But one of them would bear his children, one of them would wear the crown of Valdastien and be his wife.

"I cannot bear it!" he said aloud.

Then as if the Devil changed the scene and raised the curtain on another Act, he saw instead the women he had chosen for their attractions and who had held his interest for a short while.

Each one had seemed to have a particular perfection.

Like the paintings he had chosen to hang in the Palace to complement those that were already there, like the jewels he had given in payment for the favours he had received, and like the beauty his eyes sought in architecture, the women had been each in her individual way perfect.

It was ugliness, the King thought, that he disliked more than anything else, and he knew that he had inherited his love of beauty not only from his father but from his mother, who with her Hungarian blood had been one of the most beautiful women he had ever seen.

A brilliant rider, she had died when she was very young because like himself she preferred wild horses to those who would carry her slowly and carefully and without danger.

If she had been beautiful in life, she had also been beautiful in death, and the King knew that her loveliness was imprinted on his heart and was what he sought in every woman but had never found.

Suddenly appalled by the future that lay ahead of him, he felt as if when he had least expected it a chasm had opened at his feet.

He was no longer secure and complete in himself, but must embark on a strange, treacherous route, which he felt with an unmistakable conviction would destroy his peace of mind and contentment forever.

He rose from the chair in which he had been sitting to walk restlessly across the room and back again.

Then, as if he must escape from his own thoughts and could bear them no longer, he walked down the staircase up which he had come to the Study.

He felt for the key he had put in his waistcoat pocket, but then he hesitated.

However, he knew that although it was a palliative like wine, and a very transitory one at that, only *La Belle* could for the moment help him to forget.

*

The door of the School-Room opened but Princess Zita, who was curled up in the window-seat reading, did not turn her head.

She was in fact deep in one of her fantasy-worlds that engulfed her completely when she was reading a book, and which she entered in her thoughts at night and anytime during day when she was not interested in what was going on round her.

Now she had closed her ears against intruders and it was not until she was suddenly aware that somebody was standing beside her that she looked up and saw her elder sister, Sophie.

"What do you think has happened?" Sophie asked.

Reluctantly, because she was much more interested in what she was reading, Zita forced herself to enquire:

"What has happened?"

She did not expect it to be anything exciting, but she knew it must be at least unexpected, otherwise Sophie would not have come back to the School-Room to interrupt her.

Sophie sat down in the window-seat opposite her before she replied:

"I can hardly believe it, and yet Mama is quite certain that is why he is coming here."

"Whom are you talking about?" Zita enquired. "Who is coming?"

"King Maximilian of Valdastien has informed Papa that he is making a tour of the countries neighbouring his own and wishes to stay with us for a few nights during the course of his journey."

Sophie spoke in the rather precise, expressionless voice that she always used, but her blue eyes were very expressive, and as she finished speaking she stared at her sister apprehensively.

For a moment Zita seemed speechless, then she exclaimed:

"King Maximilian? Are you sure?"

"Quite sure," Sophie replied, "and Mama thinks he is coming to ask for my hand in marriage."

"It cannot be true!" Zita said in an incredulous tone. "We have always been told that the King is a born bachelor, determined to marry nobody, although many women would have been only too willing to share his throne with him."

Zita spoke as if to herself. Then as Sophie did not reply she went on:

"I am sure I know why he has changed his mind. Papa was speaking only the night before last to Baron Meyer about Bismarck's determination to enlarge Germany."

She paused before she went on positively:

"Yes! That will be why King Maximilian not only wants to make sure our country will stand with him against Germany but must also have an heir."

As Zita thought it out for herself she did not expect her sister to respond, knowing that Sophie was not in the least interested in politics, and not only made no attempt to listen to the conversations when their father entertained Statesmen but never even read the newspapers.

Zita enjoyed newspapers just as she enjoyed books.

She often thought that her brain was divided into two compartments: one was concerned with politics and the problems that were besetting all the countries in Europe, and the other half was filled with her fantasy-world where everything was beautiful and fairy-like.

There were no problems there, other than those that arose between the nymphs and the satyrs, the goblins and the elves, or the Sirens who with their beauty and their songs lured sailors and their ships to destruction.

This was the basis of the story she was reading when Sophie interrupted her, and for a second it was difficult to turn from the Sirens, with their long fair hair floating on the waves, to King Maximilian and his search for a wife.

Then she thought the two were not so very dissimilar after all.

Her mother, the Grand Duchess, would have been horrified to know that Zita was aware that King Maximilian had the reputation of having had under his protection the most glamourous and beautiful women who had ever appeared in the Theatre.

The Music Master who came to teach Zita to play the piano had once been a professional Concert Pianist in Paris.

He had therefore been familiar with the theatrical world, which fascinated Zita, living in the quietness of her father's country of Aldross.

"Tell me about it, tell me more, *Monsieur!*" she would beg when her lesson was over, and the Professor was only too willing to talk to such an attentive audience.

He told her about the great personalities in the Theatre, and because he went to Paris frequently to stay with two of his children who were married and lived there, Zita learnt about the latest Shows.

The Professor described the Prima Donnas who drew crowds to the Opera, the stars of the Café-Concerts, and the exquisite women who fascinated and enslaved men who spent fortunes on their gowns, jewels, carriages, horses, and anything else they desired.

Because she was so interested, the Professor brought with him the French newspapers which not only described what was seen on the stage, but gossiped frankly and often scandalously about those who filled the Boxes and constituted the audience.

King Maximilian's name appeared frequently, and to Zita he was interesting because from the portraits of him that she saw in magazines and sketches in the newspapers, he looked exactly as she thought a King should.

Exceedingly handsome, with an omnipotence and authority different from ordinary men, he was also very different from her Royal relations.

Because the Professor was carried away by his own verbosity and Zita knew how to prompt him into being very much more indiscreet than he intended, she learnt of the actresses whom the King entertained, and soon after *La Belle* was installed in the *Château* in Valdastien she was aware of it.

"Tell me what she is like," she begged the Professor.

"Beautiful, with a figure like a goddess!" the Professor replied. "When she walks onto the stage wearing a diaphanous robe which reveals the perfection of her form, the audience is silent. There is no greater compliment an actress can receive than the silence of those who are spellbound by her looks and by what she is portraying."

Zita was fascinated, but she found it hard to understand how even for a King *La Belle* could have given up the applause which the Professor had said she received night after night at the Theatre.

"But will she not feel lonely living such a quiet life in the country, which I understand is rather like ours?" Zita asked.

The Professor smiled.

"She will have the King to applaud her."

"Do you mean she will dance for him?" Zita asked.

Her words made the Professor realise that he had said far too much to a girl as young as the Princess, who should be unaware that women such as *La Belle* even existed.

"The lesson is over, Your Royal Highness," he said in a very different tone of voice. "Tomorrow we will concentrate on the compositions of Liszt and not waste time in idle gossip."

"But you must realise, Professor," Zita said in her most beguiling voice, "that when we talk together you open new horizons for me, and music, if it comes from the heart as well as the mind, cannot be constrained."

As she spoke she knew that this was the sort of language the Professor would understand and appreciate.

"Your Royal Highness is very gracious," he said. "At the same time, I should not speak of such women."

"If such women can dance as well as you say, then they are bringing beauty to the world, and that is what we all seek," Zita replied.

"That is true, very true," the Professor agreed, "but I must talk to Your Royal Highness of Rachel, who is a brilliant actress and one of the great Prima Donnas who sing the music of the Operas of which we have not yet completed our study."

"Yes, of course, Professor," Zita agreed. "At the same time, I am interested in *La Belle*, and if you can find me a picture of her in one of the newspapers or magazines, I would love to see it."

As she spoke she knew it was obvious that she was not thinking of the artistic ability of *La Belle* but of her association with King Maximilian.

"I wonder why he finds her so attractive?" Zita asked herself.

She decided she would continue to prompt the Professor into finding her a picture of *La Belle* so that she could satisfy her curiosity as to what particular allurement, apart from her dancing, had made the King take her away from Paris and keep her in Valdastien.

Now, incredibly, when she had never thought of such a thing happening, if her mother was right, King Maximilian was coming to Aldross to marry Sophie.

As the full impact of what her sister had said swept over her, Zita gave a little cry of sheer delight.

"Sophie, you are the luckiest girl in the whole world!" she said. "Have you any idea how exciting and handsome King Maximilian is? Papa said there is no Monarch in the whole Continent to equal him in looks or athletic ability. He climbed the Matterhorn one year, and you will have the most marvellous and spirited horses to ride in Valdastien."

As she spoke Zita remembered that Sophie disliked horses that were spirited and not very well bred.

It was Zita who had inherited her grandmother's horsemanship, which according to legend had made her acclaimed as an equestrienne as well as a beauty in her own country of Hungary.

"I shall not be concerned with horses," Sophie said in her prim little voice, "but with the people of Valdastien, and I shall want them to respect and admire me. I know, Zita, that I shall make a very good Queen."

"I am sure you will, dearest," Zita said impulsively, "but what is much more important than being Queen is being the wife of King Maximilian!"

Sophie was silent for a moment. Then she said:

"I do not think Mama really approves of the King, but of course she wants me to have an important position. Otherwise I think she was considering my marrying the Margrave of Baden-Baden."

Her sister made a little grimace.

"Oh, no, Sophie! He is so dull! He never says anything one remembers after he has left, or that really requires an answer after he has said it."

"I find him a nice man," Sophie objected.

As she spoke, Zita looked at her sister thoughtfully.

From all she had heard, it would be impossible to describe King Maximilian as "a nice man."

It was not only the Professor who talked about him, but also *Madame* Goutier, who came to the Palace to give the two Princesses their French lessons.

A Parisian from a good family who had married a citizen of Aldross and was now a widow, she had never lost her connection with the country of her birth.

She paid regular visits to Paris, where she had innumerable relatives who told her all the gossip.

Because Sophie found French a difficult language to learn, she never stayed to converse socially with *Madame* Goutier but always hurried away as soon as the lesson was over, leaving Zita alone with the Frenchwoman.

"Tell me the latest news from Paris, *Madame*," Zita would beg.

Because she lived a lonely life, *Madame* Goutier was only too willing to respond.

She told Zita about the Emperor and Empress, the gowns that Frederick Worth made not only for the aristocrats but also for the *demi-monde*, who were even more gorgeously clothed and jewelled than those who were entertained at the Tuileries Palace.

From *Madame* Goutier Zita learnt of the world that was not supposed to be known, and certainly not discussed, by Royal Princesses.

She heard of the wild extravagances of the women who used their beauty to lure men into throwing away fortunes just so that they could be seen with them, and because Zita was intelligent, it was not difficult for her to fill in what *Madame* Goutier left unsaid.

Because the Emperor made no secret of his love-affairs, *Madame* Goutier's daughter wrote about him often, week by week, month by month.

Prince Napoleon also flaunted his mistresses, and Zita learnt that Baron Haussmann, who had rebuilt Paris, was seen unashamedly driving in his carriage with the young actress Francine Cellier.

Too, she heard that the King of the Netherlands was infatuated with *Madame* Mustard and had spent an astronomical amount of money on her.

Because *Madame* Goutier, like the Professor, chattered without thinking, she had not the slightest idea how much of what she said was stored away in her pupil's mind.

"If only I could see Paris," Zita said to herself.

She thought she would always have to be content with just dreaming about it, cataloguing what she was told into little compartments which she could draw out like books whenever she felt that the Palace was too dull and the Court too boring to be endured.

Now, suddenly, almost like a meteor falling from the sky, the most handsome, the most dashing, and certainly the most talked-about man in Paris, King Maximilian, was to be a guest at the Palace of Aldross.

"I cannot believe it is true!" Zita exclaimed again. "And, Sophie, if you marry him it will be thrilling and exciting not only for you but for me. Promise me that you will sometimes ask me to stay with you in Valdastien, otherwise it will break my heart!"

Zita spoke pleadingly, her voice deep with the intensity of her feelings.

It was then that Sophie replied slowly, in the same expressionless voice she always used:

"No, Zita! I shall not invite you to stay with me in Valdastien or to come anywhere else with me. You are much too pretty!"

Chapter Two

How can you be so unfair, Mama?" Zita asked indignantly.

The Grand Duchess was silent, as if she was choosing her words before she said:

"This is Sophie's chance of a grand marriage, Zita, and I do not want you to interfere or spoil it for her."

"Why should I do that?"

The Grand Duchess did not answer the question. She only said:

"I am not going to argue about it. You will stay upstairs and not take part in any of the festivities arranged for King Maximilian. If you disobey me, you will have to be sent away to stay with one of our relatives."

Zita was silent, knowing that if she sometimes found the Palace gloomy, it was nothing compared to the boredom and depression she had found with her aunts and cousins who lived in much more isolated parts of the country.

Instead, she rose from the chair in which she had been sitting beside her mother and went from the room, closing the door behind her with what was suspiciously like a slam.

The Grand Duchess sighed.

She had always found Zita difficult because she was like her father, while she thought Sophie, who was amenable, quiet, and obedient, was exactly like herself.

Because the Grand Duchess was English, and a distant cousin of Queen Victoria, Zita had been speaking English while she was with her mother.

Now as she ran down the corridor towards her father's rooms she was thinking in her own language.

She burst into his Study and found him alone, as she had expected. She ran across the room to say angrily:

"I cannot believe, Papa, that it is with your approval that I am not to come to the dinner given for King Maximilian or to the Ball; in fact, I am not even to meet him while he is here!"

The Grand Duke looked up from the newspaper he was reading, and his eyes took in the fiery sparkle in Zita's green eyes, the flush on her cheeks, and the way her auburn red hair, after the haste in which she had run, seemed to be rising almost like flames over her well-shaped head.

His eyes were soft and his voice very affectionate as he said:

"I am sorry, my dearest, I was afraid it would upset you."

"Then you *did* know!" Zita said accusingly. "Oh, Papa, how could you be so unkind?"

The Grand Duke put out his hand and Zita took it to kneel down beside his chair and look up at him pleadingly.

"You know how dull it has been here lately," she said. "To dance with anybody would be exciting, but most of all with King Maximilian, whom I have always wanted to meet."

The Grand Duke's fingers tightened on hers as he said:

"I am afraid, my darling, that Sophie and your mother's decision that you will not be presented to His Majesty is the penalty you must pay for being so beautiful."

Zita stared as if she could not believe what she had heard. Then she said quickly:

"Oh, I know Sophie pretends she is jealous of me, and Mama disapproves of the way I behave when I am with you, but surely what they feel is not serious enough to have me isolated in the School-Room as if I were infectious!"

The Grand Duke smiled, but his voice was sad as he said:

"When I was told that this had been decided, I knew it would upset you. But really, dearest, there is nothing I can do about it."

"Why not?" Zita asked aggressively.

"Because," the Grand Duke explained patiently, "it is of great importance, as you will understand, that small countries like ours should unite together against the greed of Germany, and if King Maximilian should marry Sophie, it would mean that both our countries would be immeasurably stronger than we are at this moment."

As he spoke he knew that Zita would understand exactly what he was saying, because they had so often discussed the political problems of Europe.

"I thought Germany had their eyes on Austria," she said after a moment.

"Austria first, then Bavaria, then perhaps us, and after that—why not France?"

Zita drew in her breath.

She knew that her father was not speaking lightly.

It was what she had reasoned out for herself might happen if Bismarck put his ambitions into action rather than words.

She laid her cheek against her father's hand and said:

"All the same, Papa, I would still like to come to the Court Ball, and if you will allow me to attend, I shall promise not to dance with the King."

"But he might want to dance with you, my precious," the Grand Duke answered, "and that is exactly what your mother and Sophie are afraid of."

Zita did not move, but with her cheek still against her father's hand she was thinking that this was the first time any of the family had actually said that she was beautiful.

However, she would have been very stupid if she had not been aware that she closely resembled her famous Hungarian grandmother.

The former Grand Duchess had been acclaimed throughout the length and breadth of Europe and could, Zita had always been told, have made a far more important marriage than accepting the hand of the Grand Duke of Aldross.

"Your grandmama fell in love the moment she saw your grandfather," the Grand Duke had explained to Zita when she was very small and they were looking at the large portrait of the former Grand Duchess which hung in the Throne-Room.

Zita had replied almost without a pause:

"If Grandpapa looked like you, Papa, then I am not surprised. He must have been very handsome."

"Thank you, my dearest," the Grand Duke answered. "But I am glad to say that although I resemble my father, I also have inherited many characteristics of my beautiful mother, especially her love of horses and her skill in riding the most spirited animals, and I have been clever enough to create in you a replica of her."

It was perhaps because the Grand Duke had loved and admired his mother so much that he had adored his third child from the moment she was born.

He already had a son, Henrich, and a daughter, Sophie, and he had hoped, although he had not said so, that the third baby would be another son.

Yet as soon as he saw Zita he knew that somehow, in a way which he could not explain, she meant more to him than his two elder children.

As Zita grew older and became alluringly pretty with her red hair and green eyes, he had spent more time in the Nursery than he had ever done before.

When she was eight, despite the protests of the Grand Duchess, he took her away with him on one of his trips into the mountains, which had always infuriated his wife, although she could do nothing about them.

"I wish to get to know my people, and the easiest way is to move amongst them," the Grand Duke had said firmly.

Dressed in short leather trousers, a green jacket, and a Tyrolean hat, which was almost a uniform amongst the Aldross people as it was amongst the Bavarians, the Grand Duke would go off alone.

He would stay at small Inns, drink the wine that was made in the local valleys, and sing with his subjects the songs that they all knew, and which somehow expressed better than words their thoughts and their emotions.

The citizens of Aldross adored him because they thought that in consequence he understood their troubles and problems.

That he had other reasons for making these occasional excursions into the mountains just made them smile and say amongst themselves that he was "very much a man."

To Zita it was the most exciting thing in the world to go away alone with her father and look after herself without being cosseted, scolded, and interfered with by Nurses, Governesses, and of course her mother.

She and her father would ride halfway up some mountain he wished to visit; then, having left their horses, they would climb through the pine woods and onto the barren rocks and walk until Zita's legs ached.

Although she tried not to complain, sometimes she found herself forced to confess that her small legs were tired.

Then they would find a lake, and the Grand Duke would suggest that she swim in the cold clear water until she felt rested and invigorated again.

After the first trip with her father Zita learnt to swim, and on subsequent trips she swam like a small fish.

But it was an achievement she never mentioned at the Palace, knowing how much her mother would disapprove of her swimming naked, even though there was nobody but her father to see her.

Every year she and her father would go off somewhere together, and nothing the Grand Duchess could say could prevent them from slipping away for perhaps a week or ten days.

They would return brown from the sun, in radiant good health and good spirits, but they had very little to say about where they had been and what they had done.

It was when Zita was fifteen that the Grand Duchess had prevented her from going on any more trips, and no amount of pleading with her father had prevailed on him to take her.

She could not understand why a sudden embargo had been set like an iron screen on something which made her so happy and which she knew pleased her father too.

It was in fact only when she began to hear about the men in Paris who spent so much money on the beautiful ladies of the *demi-monde* that she vaguely had an idea why her father, when he did escape from the constriction of the Palace, went alone.

It was then that half-forgotten words came back to her, words which had been spoken in the past and which had meant nothing to her at the time.

"I will not have any daughter of mine associating with women like that!" she had heard the Grand Duchess say once, then she had frozen into silence as she realized Zita had come into the room.

On another occasion she had heard her mother storm:

"What sort of reputation do you think you have, consorting with creatures you meet in . . . ?"

Again there had been no end to the sentence, and gradually other memories came back to help to solve the puzzle as to why she had been left behind.

One night she had been asleep in a small room with a low ceiling and a breathtaking view of the mountain-peaks stretching away into the distance.

Because the moonlight came through the open window onto her face, Zita had stirred from a very deep sleep of sheer physical exhaustion.

She and her father had walked all day, swum in an icy cold lake, and moved on to reach an attractive little Inn high up in the mountains where he had never taken her before.

When they had arrived, a fair-haired young woman with skin like strawberries and cream, and eyes as blue as gen-

tians, came running towards them with a cry of sheer joy on
her red lips.

"You have come back!" she said almost breathlessly to the
Grand Duke. "I thought I would never see you again."

He smiled, put out his hand to touch her cheek, and said:

"I always keep my promises, Névi, and this time I have
brought my daughter to meet the prettiest woman in the
whole of Aldross!"

They had eaten a delicious dinner and Zita had been
allowed to sip a little of the special wine of the district.

Then, because she could barely keep her eyes open, she
had contentedly gone up to bed to fall asleep the moment
her head touched the pillow.

Now with the moonlight on her face she thought how
happy she was, and she was just slipping back into her
dreams when she heard a very soft, gentle laugh, then her
father's voice, deep and somehow different from any way
she had ever heard him speak before.

It seemed strange, but she was too sleepy to worry about
it, and in the morning she had forgotten what she had
heard.

When she did remember, it fitted in with her mother's
anger when her father went off on his trips, and although
Zita was no longer allowed to go with him, he continued to
go alone, and Zita was aware of how bitterly her mother
resented it.

Slowly, because children are rarely very intuitive where
their parents are concerned, she began to see her father and
mother in a very different perspective from the one with
which she had viewed them when she was a child.

She realised that their marriage had been an arranged
one and that it had been greatly to Aldross's advantage for
the Grand Duke to marry into the British Royal Family, for
it meant that they could call on a certain amount of British
friendship and support should the necessity arise.

The Grand Duchess, very English in appearance, very
stiff and shy and, as Zita thought when she grew older, cold

and unemotional, was very different from the warm, extroverted, fun-loving people of Aldross.

They laughed because they were happy, and they sang while they worked.

When it was dusk, the voices of the labourers going back to their cottages from the fields would ring out like bells and seem somehow to rise towards the snow-capped mountains as if carried on wings.

It was only this year, when she was nearly eighteen, that Zita was aware that her mother loved her father not because she was his wife but because she was a woman.

It gave her a shock when she realised inadvertently, and knew almost as if he had told her so, that while her father treated his wife with respect and attention, he was not in the least what the poets would call "in love with her."

'Oh, poor Mama!' Zita had thought to herself.

She decided then that when the occasion arose, she would categorically refuse to be pressured into marrying a man whom she did not love and who did not love her, however important he might be.

Looking at her parents with new eyes, she saw that her father, so handsome, so extremely attractive to women, must often feel desperately frustrated.

The country over which he ruled was small, and his marriage constrained him from wandering over the world as he would have liked.

He had often told Zita of his travels when he was young, of his journeys to Egypt and to Russia, and, although he was very reticent about it, the many times he had been in Paris.

When Zita questioned him as to what he had done, he talked of Rome, and when she tried to tempt him by asking artlessly about the paintings in the Tuileries Palace, he told her of those he had seen in Florence and Madrid.

Gradually, as the Professor and *Madame* Goutier made Paris come alive for her as a City of beautiful, fêted, and beguiling women, she began to understand why her father went there.

Then, after he had married, the only way he could escape to freedom and be himself was by walking in the mountains.

He loved his country, he loved the people over whom he ruled, but when there were women whose eyes sparkled and whose arms went out to him the moment he appeared, it was certainly not in his nature to turn his back on them.

"I am sorry for Papa too," Zita told herself.

She was also sorry for herself, because she was no longer allowed to accompany him but had to stay in the Palace with her mother.

At those times the Grand Duchess was more fault-finding than usual, and the whole Court seemed to be enveloped in a heavy gloom that was like a fog until her father returned.

As if he followed her thoughts and understood that his favourite child was feeling as frustrated as he often felt himself, the Grand Duke said:

"I tell you what I will do, dearest: I will agree with your mother that you will not put in an appearance during the King's visit and that he shall not meet you, on the condition that when he leaves, you and I go on one of our trips together into the mountains."

Zita raised her eyes to his and there seemed to be sunshine in her face.

"Do you mean that, Papa? It would be wonderful! I cannot tell you how much I have missed our times together."

"I have missed them too, my dearest," the Grand Duke said, "but your mother was adamant that you were too old to accompany me, and I must admit that I think she was right."

"But this time she will have to make an exception," Zita said. "Swear to me that you will keep your promise and not let Mama make you change your mind!"

"I promise," the Grand Duke said. "I want to climb a mountain at the very end of the range where I have not been for at least ten years. It will be exciting to show it to you."

"I would love that, Papa. And let us stay away a long time,

because it will be so marvellous for me to have you all to myself."

The Grand Duke bent forward and kissed her.

"I love you, my Zita," he said, "and I want you to have anything and everything that would make you happy. But it is not always easy for me—you know that."

"Yes, I know, Papa, and let us hope that the King will marry Sophie, so that we can stop worrying not only about whom she can marry but also about Aldross being eaten up by that monster Bismarck."

The Grand Duke laughed before he said:

"Amen to that! And now, dearest, try not to make a fuss about anything until the Royal visit is over. It makes things so much easier for me if your mother is in a good temper."

"I will try to keep out of her way," Zita said simply. "I always seem to upset her, although I cannot think why."

The Grand Duke could have answered in one word: "jealousy." But he knew it would be disloyal to say so, and therefore he kept silent.

After Zita had kissed him affectionately and left him, he sat for a long time thinking about her.

He knew that living quietly in the Palace and being constantly found fault with by her mother, Zita had no idea of her beauty or how fascinating men would find her.

He remembered as a boy the expression he had noted in the eyes of men of all ages, all classes, and all descriptions when they had looked at his mother, and he thought he had already seen that same look amongst the elderly Courtiers of the Palace whenever Zita appeared.

He was quite certain that if King Maximilian was thinking of taking a wife to Valdastien he would certainly prefer Zita to Sophie.

But it was only fair that the elder sister should be married first, and as Sophie was twenty it was time she was settled and off their hands.

The difficulty was that, with the exception of the Margrave of Baden-Baden, there were very few young men of

Royal blood who came to Aldross or invited them to visit
their own countries.

The Grand Duchess had already said despairingly that
Sophie would die an old maid if she did not do something
about it.

"What can I do?" the Grand Duke had asked. "I cannot
conjure up eligible Kings or Princes as if they were mush-
rooms, and you know as well as I do, Louise, that all the
adjacent countries to this, with the exception of Valdastien,
are ruled by married Monarchs and their children are
mostly still in the Nursery."

"It is no use thinking of King Maximilian," the Grand
Duchess had said sharply at the time. "He wastes his time
with the sort of creatures you find attractive and who are
not spoken of in any lady's Drawing-Room!"

"I hear the woman he has with him now at Valdastien has
a figure that leaves any man who sees her speechless!" the
Grand Duke replied, as if he were talking to himself.

He knew as soon as he had spoken that he had made a
mistake, for the Grand Duchess merely lifted her chin dis-
dainfully and walked from the room without speaking.

This meant, the Grand Duke knew, that she would sulk
for the next twenty-four hours and the atmosphere at the
next few meals could be colloquially described as one you
could "cut with a knife!"

He picked up his newspaper from where he had put it
down when Zita entered the room, and as he did so he said
to himself:

"Poor Maximilian! He will find when he is married that
Les Belles who have entertained him in the past will be in
Paris while he will be incarcerated, for better or for worse,
in Valdastien!"

*

Although Zita tried not to upset her mother, as she had
promised her father, she found it intolerable to hear and

feel the excitement running through the Palace and know that she could not be part of it.

Sophie had to have new gowns and the dressmakers came and went.

The covers were taken from the furniture in the Ball-Room, the floor was polished, the gold and white walls were cleaned so that they shone as if they had been decorated only yesterday.

Flowers were brought in from the greenhouses and arranged by the gardeners until not only the Ball-Room but almost every part of the Palace looked like a bower of blossoms.

"I cannot think, Papa, why our rooms cannot always look beautiful just like this for us," Zita said at luncheon, "instead of everything being done for a passing visitor, who will doubtless not appreciate it as much as we do."

"You certainly have a point there," the Grand Duke replied.

He always enjoyed arguments with his youngest daughter, which stimulated his mind and hers, and that they often took opposite sides just for the fun of it was something the Grand Duchess could never understand.

"At the same time," he went on, "if the unusual was the usual and commonplace, you would not appreciate it so much."

Zita's eyes sparkled, and she was just about to reply, when the Grand Duchess said:

"That is enough of your ridiculous ideas, Zita! And try not to bother your father with stupid questions. We have a lot to do and a great deal to plan before His Majesty arrives tomorrow."

"At what time are you expecting him, Mama?" Sophie enquired.

Because it was her favourite who asked the question, the Grand Duchess was prepared to answer.

"You will find a programme of the events on my desk,"

she said. "The King will already have left by now on the first part of his journey. He is staying the night with one of his friends who has a Castle not far from our border."

"When shall we see him?" Sophie asked eagerly.

"Your father will greet His Majesty at The Inn of the Golden Cross at eleven o'clock tomorrow morning and bring him to the Palace with an escort of Cavalry."

"And where shall we be?"

"We will be waiting for him here," the Grand Duchess replied, "and you must wear that pretty pink gown in which I am sure he will think you look just like a rose."

As Sophie had dull brown hair and a solemn, unsmiling expression, she could never at any time have looked like a flower.

Zita repressed a desire to laugh at her mother's uncharacteristically poetical remark, then she caught her father's eye.

Instead she said, because she felt it would help:

"Do tell the hairdresser, Sophie, to arrange your hair more softly. If it curls round your face instead of being brushed back it will be very flattering and, as Mama said, will make you look like a flower."

"When I want your opinion, Zita, I will ask for it," the Grand Duchess said crushingly.

She rose from the table and put out her hand towards her elder daughter.

"Come along, Sophie, we have masses of things to do before tomorrow, and I do not wish you to listen to anybody's advice except mine."

They went from the room and Zita gave a little sigh and looked at her father.

There was no need for words. They both knew what the other was thinking, and the Grand Duke laid his hand over hers.

"Think of the fun we will have together in the mountains," he said gently.

Upstairs in her bedroom, because it was the only place in which she did not feel irritated by the preparations for the King, Zita stood at the window, wondering how she could have a glimpse of him while he was in the Palace.

However, the Grand Duchess had reiterated over and over again how she was to stay upstairs in the School-Room, which had formerly been called the Nursery and later "Their Royal Highnesses Sitting-Room."

But it still remained in their own minds the Nursery.

The room had been redecorated and the windows framed by crisp muslin curtains, and the furniture had been made and carved locally.

Yet it always seemed to Zita to contain the doll's house which had belonged to her and Sophie, the rocking-horse on which Henrich had ridden for hours on end, his toy fort, which they were not allowed to touch, and a number of dolls which he teased them by hiding or, when he was in a temper, breaking.

'I suppose when we leave these rooms and live in Palaces of our own we will feel grown-up,' Zita thought with perception.

She wondered if Sophie would be happy in Valdastien with the ghosts of *La Belle* and other women like her peeping round every corner.

Then she thought it would not be Sophie who would see them—for probably she would never be aware of their existence—but the King.

She wondered if he would feel frustrated as her father did, and if he would have to resort to climbing his own mountains and disappearing into his own forests instead of going to Paris and enjoying himself as he obviously did now.

It was difficult to guess what he would think or feel when all she had to guide her were the stories she had heard from the Professor and *Madame* Goutier, and the pictures she had seen in the newspapers and magazines, which she was sure were very bad likenesses of him.

It was then that she told herself she would see him and that nobody would stop her!

"Even if I have to stand in the roadway as he drives by, I will have a look at him!" she said determinedly.

Suddenly an idea came to her which she knew was outrageous and very naughty, but which she could not help feeling would be very exciting.

"Nobody will ever know," she said aloud.

At the same time, she was well aware that what she was planning would horrify her mother if she had any inkling of it.

*

Nobody paid any attention to Zita the night before the King's arrival, but if they had, they might have noticed that she was very silent and engrossed in her thoughts.

At the same time, her eyes had a light in them which the Grand Duke might have recognised as being the same as that which shone in his mother's eyes when she was planning something particularly adventurous.

The Princess Ilena, as she had been called before she married, had scandalised the old-fashioned Dowagers of her father's Court, but the people had admired her for her courage as well as for her beauty.

This was something that Zita thought her grandmother would have dared to do, for, like the wild horses she rode, she had a spirit that was impossible to quench or destroy.

"I will do it!" Zita decided before she went to bed, and to her mother's relief she retired early, saying that she had a slight headache.

Upstairs in her bedroom, anybody watching her undress would have been surprised to see her laying out her riding-habit.

She also took some time in packing up a parcel of clothes that she would carry in the same way as she carried those she took when she went off with her father—attached to the saddle of her horse.

Because she was too excited to sleep, Zita dozed for a little while but kept waking to look at the sky through the open window from which she had pulled back the curtains.

Then as the stars began to fade and the first faint show of the dawn appeared over the distant horizon she rose and dressed quickly; then, carrying the bundle she had parcelled up the night before, she slipped down a side staircase which led to the stables.

She moved quietly past two sleepy sentries who were on duty at one of the more important doors of the Palace and reached the stables without being seen.

She was well aware that there would be nobody about at this time of the morning, and she walked into the nearest harness room to pick up her horse's saddle.

Then she hurried towards the small paddock where the horse she loved more than almost anything else in the world was kept in the summer.

She gave a faint whistle and Pegasus came trotting towards her eagerly. She slipped the bridle over his head and flung the saddle onto his back.

If there was one thing her trips with her father had taught her, it was to be completely self-sufficient where it concerned either herself or her horse.

"How can you want to cope with your horse without a groom?" Sophie had asked scornfully.

But Zita had known it was far more exciting to be alone with her father on such trips than to be accompanied by servants who would not only talk about what they did but doubtless would be very critical of the discomforts which Zita and her father ignored.

She tightened his girth while Pegasus stood quite still for her to do so. Then, without the need of anybody to assist her, she seemed almost to fly into the saddle.

Twisting between the trees until they were out of the Palace grounds, Zita galloped Pegasus wildly over the meadowland in the direction in which she wished to go, avoiding the houses and the roads.

They travelled over lush grass that was thick with alpine flowers of pink, white, mauve, and red, which grew more vivid every moment as the light increased and the first rays of the sun turned the snow on the peaks of the mountains to gold.

It was not far to The Inn of the Golden Cross, which Zita was heading for, and when she arrived it was still so early in the morning that there was only one sleepy ostler moving about in the courtyard into which she rode her horse.

When she appeared to know her way about, he took no further notice of her, and she put Pegasus into an empty stall and removed her bundle from his back.

Then she went in through a side door which fortunately was open and up a narrow staircase which led her to the back of the hostelry, where the Proprietor's private apartments were located.

She walked along an uncarpeted passage, knocked perfunctorily at the door at the far end of it, and when there was no reply she lifted the latch.

She looked inside and saw a young woman sitting on the bed in her nightgown, rubbing the sleep from her eyes.

Zita walked in.

"Good-morning, Gretel!"

The woman looked at her in astonishment, then cried:

"Princess! What are you doing here?"

Zita shut the door and put her finger to her lips.

"Hush!" she cautioned. "I am not a Princess at the moment, but your friend who has come to visit you from the town."

Gretel, who was a pretty, buxom girl, a little older than Zita, with apple cheeks and china-blue eyes, stared at her in astonishment.

"I thought I'd never see you again!" she said. "I thought your father would visit us, but I didn't expect you."

"I was not allowed to come."

Zita sat down on the edge of the bed and went on:

"Listen, Gretel, I want your help."

"I will do anything you ask me," Gretel replied. "How pretty you have grown! I have seen you in the distance driving through the streets, but you are even prettier close to."

"Thank you," Zita said with a smile. "But it is because I am so pretty, Gretel, that I am not allowed to see King Maximilian when he comes to stay at the Palace today."

"Not allowed to see him? Why not?"

"My mother and father are hoping he will marry my sister."

Gretel laughed.

"There's no need to say any more," she said. "You're very much prettier than your sister, as you well know."

When Zita was travelling with her father it was understood that they were incognito and everybody talked to them as if they were their equals. Sometimes the Grand Duke even pretended to himself that his subjects did not recognise him.

Of course they did, for he was far too handsome, too loved, and too admired for them not to do so.

But because it pleased him they addressed him as *"Mein Herr,"* and Zita was just "Zita," a pretty child whom the old men patted on the head and carved wooden toys to amuse her.

"What do you want me to do?" Gretel asked.

"I read the programme that was being prepared for the King," Zita said, "and learnt that it has been arranged he should come here for an hour."

Gretel nodded.

"Yes, we have a room ready and waiting for him."

"I have worked out," Zita continued, "that he will arrive here on horseback and in ordinary clothes, but because he is to drive on with Papa in an open carriage, he will have to change into uniform."

"I don't know about that," Gretel said. "We were just told to have the best bedroom ready for him."

"Is that the one in which Papa always stays?" Zita enquired.

Gretel nodded.

"Well, when he goes up there alone," Zita said, "I want you to offer him a cup of coffee or some wine, and when you bring it up, I will carry it in to him."

Gretel looked at her in astonishment.

"Why should you want to do that?"

"Because it is the only chance I shall ever have of seeing him properly," Zita replied. "Oh, Gretel, you have to help me! I want so much to see him, and it would be too depressing if he goes away and I never even catch a glimpse of him except for the top of his head from my bedroom window."

"If he's wearing a plumed helmet you won't see very much," Gretel said with a smile.

"No, that is what I thought," Zita answered. "That is why you have to help me, and I have brought a dress with me like the one I used to wear when I went away with Papa."

She went on:

"Actually, it is not the same one, because I cannot get into it, but I managed to persuade one of the housemaids to buy me a new one in town without Mama knowing. And listen, Gretel, I am sure we will soon be coming to see you, because Papa has promised to take me into the mountains with him after the King has left."

"I'm glad about that!" Gretel exclaimed. "And you must come here! You know how we love having you."

"It used to be such fun!" Zita said. "Do you remember the night I danced for your guests, and not only did they clap but they threw flowers at me as if they were bouquets."

"They thought you were marvellous!" Gretel said. "So did I!"

"I must have been about nine when that happened."

Gretel gave a little laugh.

"I remember one night a man who really didn't know who you were tried to kiss you, and you poured beer over his head! Everybody laughed and teased him so that he went away in a huff!"

"Luckily Papa was doing something else and did not see what was happening," Zita said, "or I have a feeling he would not have let me talk so freely to strangers as I was allowed to do."

"You were always so pretty, that was the trouble," Gretel said.

"Yes, that was the trouble," Zita agreed, "and that is the trouble now. I shall never be allowed to see the King unless you help me."

"What if he knows who you are?" Gretel suggested.

"Why should he?" Zita replied. "I assure you, at home they are not even going to mention that I exist in case he asks to see me. Sophie wants him to herself, and that is what she is going to have, but I just want to have one tiny peep at him before he rides away at Papa's side with everybody cheering except me."

Zita thought for a second. Then she said:

"I cannot see how there would be any harm in it, and there is no reason for anybody in the Inn to know I am here, except you."

"Who saw you when you came in?"

"Only an ostler. I do not know him by sight and he paid no attention to me."

"That'll be Carl. He's always up early, and he's rather stupid."

"If anybody asks whose horse it is in the stable, just say you had a friend to visit you," Zita continued, "but I do not suppose they will ask many questions."

"No, of course not," Gretel agreed. "Let's have a look at your dress, and I'd better put on some clothes or I'll get into trouble."

As Zita undid her bundle, Gretel dressed quickly, putting on clothes of the same sort as Zita had brought with her.

It was the national costume of Aldross and was almost identical to those of all the other countries in that part of Europe.

There was a very full red skirt over a number of stiffly starched petticoats, a prettily embroidered white blouse which had over it a black velvet corset which laced down the front, and a ribbon sash.

All that was missing from Zita's costume was the white apron that Gretel wore when she was working.

"I could not ask the maid to buy me that," Zita explained, "she might have thought it strange."

"I'm sure she would have," Gretel agreed. "She wouldn't expect her Royal Highness to be handing round the coffee and pouring out glasses of wine!"

She went to a chest-of-drawers in the corner of the room and fetched a little apron very much like her own, except that it was edged with lace.

"This is my best," she said. "I was going to wear it for His Majesty, but your need is greater than mine."

"Thank you, Gretel," Zita said. "Any tip he gives me will be yours."

Gretel laughed.

"I don't expect much in the way of a tip. I've always found that the grand ones who come through here think their presence is enough benefit to those who wait on them."

Zita laughed.

"Well, we will find out exactly what the King is like once we have met him," she said, "whether he is generous or stingy, gracious or ungracious. Approaching him as a serving-maid will be very different, I am sure, from meeting him on equal terms."

"You'll get into trouble if you're found out, and so shall I!" Gretel said.

"You can put all the blame on me," Zita said. "But if we

are clever there should be no reason why anyone should know anything about it, and I shall have caught a glimpse of His Majesty King Maximilian off-guard, which I feel will be very revealing!"

Chapter Three

WHEN she was dressed Gretel went downstairs to fetch Zita some steaming black coffee and hot croissants straight from the oven.

"It's all right," she said when she brought them to the bedroom. "Nobody's going to worry about you. They're all in a fever of excitement getting ready for the King."

She then showed Zita to the room across the passage, where she could watch the King's entourage as it came through Valdastien towards Aldross.

The Inn of the Golden Cross had been built, as its Proprietor claimed, exactly on the boundary.

"I am astride two nations," he would say as he stood at the bar with his hands on his hips, looking like Falstaff.

One reason why the Inn was patronised by the citizens both of Aldross and of Valdastien was that it was at the foot of one of the highest and most popular mountains in Aldross.

That was why the Grand Duke so often stopped at the Inn when he was on his climbing expeditions.

It was also, Zita observed, a jovial place where everybody seemed to be laughing or singing, and the food was certainly better than the fare at many other Inns of the same sort.

Having finished her coffee and croissants, she took off her riding-habit and dressed herself in the national costume, which was very becoming.

Fortunately, one of the housemaids at the Palace was an intelligent woman who had understood exactly what Zita wanted and was also prepared to keep the purchase secret.

"When all the festivities are over, Maria," Zita had told her confidentially, "I am going away with Papa into the mountains. As you know, he likes to think that nobody recognises us, so I must look like a peasant."

Maria had laughed.

"That's the last thing you look, Your Royal Highness, and everybody recognises the Grand Duke, even though they pretend otherwise."

"I know that," Zita replied with a smile, "but all I am concerned with at the moment is that I shall be with him and get away from here and being scolded every time I open my mouth."

"It's a real shame Your Royal Highness is not allowed to go to the Ball!" Maria exclaimed. "Everybody downstairs says how you'd be the loveliest person present, and it's too bad you have to miss it all."

"I know," Zita sighed, "but if Princess Sophie marries the King, then we will have a Royal Wedding, and that will be very exciting!"

As she spoke, she saw the expression on Maria's face, and knew that the maid thought it was very unlikely that this would happen.

Because Zita knew it would be very indiscreet for her to discuss her sister with one of the servants, she had quickly changed the subject.

Now when she had finished dressing she looked in the small mirror that Gretel had in her room and arranged her hair as the peasant-girls did, with ribbons which fell down to her shoulders.

She had been very careful to order these to be of green, yellow, and blue, which would not clash with the colour of her hair, and when the arrangement was finished she thought that it was in fact a very becoming head-dress.

By now there was a noise and bustle downstairs which told her that everybody was up and making feverish preparations for their distinguished guest.

She had learnt from the programme which she had read when it was on her mother's desk that the two Rulers were to meet in private inside the Inn.

When they had exchanged greetings and taken a glass of wine together, the King's escort would return home, and the Rulers of Aldross and Valdastien, driving in an open carriage escorted by a squadron of Cavalry, would travel down the decorated road towards the Capital.

First the King would be greeted by the Prime Minister and the Members of the Cabinet, then by the Civic Mayor and the Aldermen of the City.

After that they were to proceed to the Palace, where the Grand Duchess and Sophie would be waiting for them.

As Zita remembered what was to happen, she thought with a smile that King Maximilian would doubtless find it very boring.

"I am sure it is something he has done thousands of times," she told herself, "and he would much rather be driving in the Bois de Boulogne with a lovely lady beside him, looking forward to a *tête-á-tête* this evening and perhaps dining with her in one of the smart Restaurants in Paris where there is both dancing and a Café-Concert."

These were of course the entertainments that *Madame Goutier* and the Professor had described to her, and because she elaborated and coloured them in her imagination, she could almost see them happening.

"I know that is what the King would really enjoy," she decided.

Because she thought it was getting late, she left Gretel's bedroom and walked across the passage to enter an empty room with a window that looked directly into Valdastien.

It was not unlike Aldross in that there were high, snow-capped mountains and between them a rich valley where horses could gallop freely over grass colourful with wild flowers.

The great difference between the two countries was that

Valdastien was fertilised through the very centre of it by a
wide river which not only ensured that their crops were
productive but could also carry barges filled with merchan-
dise from Valdastien directly to the sea.

This made the country much more prosperous than
some of its neighbours and naturally evoked a certain
amount of envy.

'It would certainly be to Aldross's advantage if there was a
link between our two countries,' Zita thought, 'and of
course if Sophie marries the King we shall be in a much
stronger position to stand up against Germany.'

She moved a hard chair to the window and sat on it,
leaning her elbows on the sill to look down the narrow,
dusty road which ran from the hillside into the valley and
along which the King would ride.

By now, Zita thought, the housemaid who usually called
her would be aware that she was not in the Palace and she
would doubtless report her absence to her Lady-in-Waiting.

She thought it might have been wiser to take Maria into
her confidence. Then she decided that because her riding-
habit was missing and her boots were not in their usual
place, Maria would think she had gone riding.

The Lady-in-Waiting, Baroness Mekszath, whom she
shared with Sophie, would be far too busy dolling herself up
to be in attendance when the King arrived for her to worry
over what had happened to her other charge.

"When I get home," Zita decided, "I will just say I went
for a ride. Nobody can blame me for wanting to do something on my own when I have been excluded from all the
excitement they are able to enjoy."

As she thought again somewhat resentfully of the way she
had been treated, she saw in the far distance a cloud of dust
and felt her heart leap with excitement.

It was difficult to see clearly for some time.

Then at last she realised there was not one carriage but a
number of them, and when they came nearer still she saw,

as she had expected, that the King was riding ahead with a number of attendants also on horseback.

Behind them came the carriages bringing the Dignitaries of Valdastien, who would bid him farewell at the boundary, and after them followed the luggage with the valets and footmen who attended His Majesty.

Because there seemed so much luggage, Zita thought how much more pleasant it was to travel as she and her father would do when all this was over.

All they required would be rolled up in two bundles, one attached to each of their saddles, with just a few small objects in the saddle-bags themselves.

"We will be free, free of all that kowtowing and: 'Yes, Your Majesty!' and 'No, Your Royal Highness!' " she said to herself.

The cavalcade came nearer still, and now Zita could pick out quite clearly which rider was the King.

It was easy because he was a dominating and distinguished figure, even though he was wearing plain riding-clothes that were indistinguishable from those of his companions.

Then Zita thought as she watched them drawing nearer and nearer that she would have known he was somebody of authority even if she had seen him standing in a crowd.

He rode at a sharp pace although the Inn was in sight, and only when they reached it and he was aware that a welcoming party was waiting for him did he say something to one of the men beside him and draw in his horse.

The main door of the Inn was obscured from Zita's view because the building had been erected right on the frontier, so that part of it lay in one country and part in the other.

The King therefore disappeared from her view before she could really see him as closely as she wished to do.

Then there was only the dust as the carriages drew to a standstill, before they could move on to the front door.

Zita watched for a moment or two, then with a little

murmur of excitement because the moment was growing near when she would see the King, she followed Gretel's instructions and moved along the passage to the front of the Inn.

She knew which bedroom the King was to use, and Gretel had shown her a small room opposite it which was occupied usually by a servant or a traveller who could not pay much money, but which at this moment was empty.

Zita slipped inside, leaving the door ajar so that she could hear the sound of voices downstairs, and as they rose louder and louder she was aware that the King was being escorted into the Inn by the Proprietor.

Then she decided that he must be having a drink with his own people before they left him, because she thought she could hear the clink of glasses and the popping of corks, although it might have been her imagination.

At any rate, she was certain that they would be toasting the King and wishing him luck on the journey that lay ahead of him.

She had already worked out for herself the other countries he might visit in search of a wife, if Sophie did not come up to his expectations.

It was obviously to his advantage to marry somebody who lived "next door," so he might visit Bosnia, Serbia, Bulgaria, and perhaps even Rumania, although that was much farther away from Valdastien.

Another of the countries could be Hungary, and Zita was certain that there he could find a Hungarian Princess who, if nothing else, would appreciate the Valdastien horses.

When she had questioned her father as to whether there were many eligible brides in these countries, he had been very vague.

"I really do not know the answer to that, my dearest," he had replied. "All I do know is that there are few countries with eligible bachelors for you two girls."

"That makes it all the more important for Sophie to

capture the King," Zita remarked. "At least he is an eligible bachelor, and from all I have heard, he is very attractive."

The Grand Duke was silent for a moment before he remarked:

"Attractive men do not always make good husbands."

Zita was about to make a complimentary reply when she thought that if she was honest, although her father outwardly was a most attentive husband, he failed his wife in that he had never given her his heart.

'But that is something no-one can give without love,' she thought to herself, 'and it is also something which does not obey orders even when they are given by Kings or Queens.'

She began to laugh at her own fantasy.

Then as if her father realised they were walking on delicate ground, he changed the subject to talk about something else.

Zita was suddenly aware that somebody was coming up the uncarpeted wooden stairs and she pushed the door against which she was standing a little farther to, so that there was only a tiny crack for her to see through.

As she had expected, she saw a man who was obviously a valet, followed by the porter from the Inn carrying a small trunk.

"I'll unpack for His Majesty," she heard the valet say as they disappeared into the bedroom, "and when I have repacked it with the clothes he's wearing now, you can take it down and put it on the back of the carriage which will follow His Majesty to the City."

The words were spoken in the somewhat grandiose manner of a Palace servant who thinks himself immeasurably superior to all lesser servants.

There was the thump of a trunk being put down on the floor and the noise of straps being undone, and Zita could visualise the King's uniform being taken out and laid on the bed.

The porter had already gone back down the stairs and now there was only the valet in the bedroom.

It struck Zita for the first time that she would not see the King alone.

She had forgotten that he would not dress himself, and although it rather spoilt her plan if there was a servant present when she saw him, it was not really important.

Then she was half-afraid that the valet might take the coffee from her and she would get no farther than the door of the room.

She was wondering what she should do if that happened, when there was the sound of much lighter footsteps coming up the stairs, but which had an authoritative sound about them which made her sure it was the King.

She had a quick glimpse of his broad shoulders as he went to the bedroom, and just as he was about to shut the door Gretel came running up the stairs after him to say:

"Your Majesty!"

The King stopped and turned around.

"I have something to ask Your Majesty," Gretel said breathlessly. "Would you like coffee, or perhaps a glass of wine?"

The King seemed to consider the question. Then he replied:

"A cup of coffee would be very acceptable."

"I will fetch it immediately, Your Majesty!"

Gretel bobbed him a curtsey and ran down the stairs again and the King shut the door of the bedroom.

It seemed to Zita a long time before Gretel came up again with a tray in her hands, but actually it was only a few minutes.

Zita opened the door and took the tray from her.

"I forgot he would have his valet with him!" she whispered.

Gretel raised her eyes.

"I never thought you would want to speak to him alone!"

"I may not get the chance to speak to him at all," Zita replied, "if the valet takes the tray from me."

Gretel understood, and there was a smile on her face as she crossed the passage and knocked on the door of the King's bedroom.

It was opened by the valet.

"Excuse me," Gretel said, "but a gentleman in one of the carriages wishes to speak to you."

"To me?" the valet questioned in surprise.

"Yes, he's found something which he thinks has been overlooked and His Majesty might want to take with him."

"I will see to it."

He turned back to say:

"Excuse me, Your Majesty, but I must go downstairs."

He passed Gretel without speaking, and she winked at Zita before she followed him.

Zita drew in her breath, then carrying the tray carefully she walked to the open door and knocked on it.

"Your Majesty's coffee," she said in a soft voice.

"Bring it in," the King replied.

She entered the room to find him standing in front of a mirror above a chest-of-drawers, brushing his hair with two ivory-back brushes with the Royal Monogram on them in gold.

He was wearing the long black trousers with a red stripe down the seam, which was part of his uniform, and a white linen shirt.

It made his shoulders seem very broad and his hips very narrow, and Zita, who had often seen her father brushing his hair in the same way when he was partially dressed, had always thought it made a man look exceedingly attractive.

Now as she walked across the room she set the tray down on a round table in the bow-window. It was where her father always had his.

Also on the tray was a plate containing some warm croissants of the type she herself had eaten and a pat of butter in a glass dish.

The King still had his back to her, and after a moment, because she was determined that he should turn round, she asked:

"Shall I pour out the coffee, Your Majesty?"

Without really thinking about it, she addressed him in his own language.

Languages had never been any difficulty to Zita, and she spoke not only English, French, German, and Italian perfectly, but she had also learned from her father the languages of the countries which bordered Aldross, which were, he had always said, part of their blood.

They were all based on a mixture of German and Hungarian, but each had a variation that was all its own and an inflection which was particularly characteristic of its people.

The King put down his hair-brushes.

"You are obviously one of my subjects," he said with a faint smile.

Then as he looked at her he was suddenly still.

She was standing in the sunshine that came through the bow-window and it picked out the red in her hair, making it glow like the flames from a fire, and her skin was dazzlingly white.

Because she was excited by what she was doing, her eyes seemed to sparkle like emeralds.

For Zita too the King was a surprise, being quite different from what she had expected.

For one thing, he was better-looking and far younger than he appeared in the portraits she had seen of him, but it was not merely his physical appearance that surprised her.

Because she was always intuitive about people, she could feel, as it were, vibrations coming from him that made him different, not because he was a King but because he was different from anybody she had ever met before.

There was, she thought, something magnetic about him, and as she stared at him without really meaning to, she realised that he was staring at her in exactly the same way.

Then, as if he recovered first, the King said:

"You have not answered my question."

For a second Zita could not remember what it was. Then she said:

"No, I am not from your country, Your Majesty, but from Aldross."

"But you have learnt my language."

"It is not so very different from ours."

"I agree there are many similarities," he said, "but you speak it as if you have lived in Valdastien all your life, although that cannot have been very long."

"I have never visited Your Majesty's country, but I long to do so."

"I hope when you do you will not be disappointed."

Zita thought they were speaking to each other in a very strange manner. It was almost as if the words came to their lips, and yet their thoughts were elsewhere.

Then it was as if having looked at the King, Zita could not take her eyes from his.

Because she was half-afraid he would dismiss her, and she wanted to go on talking to him, she said quickly:

"Your Majesty must drink your coffee while it is hot, and I hope you will try the croissants. They are delicious."

"I am sure they are," the King answered, "and perhaps an appreciation of good food and good wine is something our two countries share."

"Then, as Your Majesty said to me, I hope you are not disappointed."

As Zita spoke she picked up the heavy coffee-pot and poured the coffee into the large cup, aware as she did so that the King was watching her in a way that made her feel shy.

At the same time she was excited because she was seeing him and talking to him, and even if she would never be able to do so again, at least she would have this to remember.

"What is your name?" the King asked unexpectedly.

Because she was so bemused with what was happening, Zita told the truth.

"Zita."

Even as she spoke she wondered frantically if she had been indiscreet.

Then she remembered that officially she was always referred to as "Princess Teresa," which was her first name.

"Zita" was used only by the family and by the people of Aldross who lived in the vicinity of the Palace, because for them it was a term of affection.

"A pretty name," the King observed, "for a very pretty person."

Zita looked at him in surprise.

She could hardly believe that King Maximilian of Valdastien would flirt with the waitress of an Inn.

Then she asked herself why he should not do so.

It was the sort of remark her father would have made in his jovial, friendly fashion to any pretty woman he encountered on his travels when he was thought to be incognito.

The King came nearer to the table.

"I have always believed," he said, "that red hair was only to be found on the ladies of Hungary."

Zita smiled.

"My grandmother was Hungarian, Your Majesty."

"That accounts for it," the King said, as if he was pleased at having been right, "and I presume she also had green eyes?"

Zita smiled again but did not answer, and after a moment the King said:

"Do you like working here?"

"I have not been here long."

"I should have thought with your looks . . . " the King began.

Then he stopped as if he commanded himself to do so, and picking up the cup of coffee that Zita had poured out for him he sipped. But while he did so his eyes were still on her face.

Zita waited and thought that if she behaved correctly she should withdraw, but she wanted desperately to stay.

"How old are you?" the King asked.

"Nearly eighteen, Your Majesty."

"And this is the first time you have been out to work?"

"It is gracious of Your Majesty to be interested."

The King put down the cup of coffee.

"I am interested," he said, "because I appreciate beauty, and it seems to me that yours is wasted in a place like this when you . . . "

Again he stopped speaking.

"When I . . . what, Your Majesty?" Zita prompted.

" . . . When you could do a great many other things," the King finished, "or perhaps they would spoil you, and that would be a pity."

"What other things does Your Majesty think I could do?"

As she spoke she thought that this was a fascinating conversation to be having with a King who had no idea who she was.

It was almost as if she were talking with her father when they sought for words with which they could puzzle or perhaps confuse each other as if in a game.

"Can you dance?" the King asked.

"But of course!" Zita replied. "I can dance like a gypsy or, if Your Majesty prefers, the folk-dancers of Aldross, who I imagine are very much the same as the folk-dancers you have in your own country."

She spoke almost teasingly, as she might have spoken to her father, and the King looked at her sharply before he said:

"I find you very puzzling. You speak in an educated voice, and both your grammar and the way you phrase your sentences shows that you have a command of my language which I certainly did not expect to find in a . . . "

He paused for the right description, but before he could speak Zita added:

" . . . In a peasant!"

The King laughed.

"You do not look like a peasant! Now speak to me in what you tell me is your own language."

"What would Your Majesty like me to say?" Zita asked in the language of Aldross.

"It does not matter. Go on talking until I can decide something."

She gave a little laugh. Then because she thought it would puzzle him even more, she said in perfect Parisian French:

"Perhaps if we are entering a language-contest, I should be allowed to hear how fluent Your Majesty is in the language of the gayest Capital in the world."

The King stared at her in undisguised astonishment. Then he said harshly:

"Is this some joke? Who are you? An actress? Who has sent you to talk to me?"

It was a reaction she had not expected, and Zita said quickly:

"It is nothing like that. I just happen, Your Majesty, to be good at languages, and I have taken the trouble to learn them."

"Is that the truth?"

"I promise you . . . it is."

She looked up at him almost pleadingly, anxious not to annoy him, not to spoil what had been a few moments of delight before he had become suspicious of her.

Her green eyes met his grey ones, then it was difficult to look away or even to remember what they were saying.

As if the King suddenly remembered that time was passing, he said:

"I want to see you again, Zita, and continue this conversation. Before I leave Aldross I will send you a message saying where we can meet."

He paused before he added:

"I will either come here or arrange for you to come to me. Are you willing to do that?"

Zita stared at him, not knowing what to say. Then hesitatingly, because somehow her mind would not work, she replied:

"It . . . might be . . . impossible."

"Nothing is impossible," the King said firmly, "and although we will have to be very discreet, I am determined, completely determined, that we will not only meet but that you shall explain three mysteries to me."

"What . . . are . . . they?"

"The colour of your hair, the expression in your eyes, and your aptitude for languages."

There was a mocking note in his voice, but Zita knew he was speaking seriously.

Then before she could reply there was the sound of footsteps outside the door and the King's valet came hurrying into the room.

"I don't understand who it was who sent for me, Your Majesty," he said. "The carriages have left, and if anything's been forgotten there's nothing I can do about it now."

The King did not answer. He was lifting his tunic off the bed and the valet hurriedly helped him into it.

"They asked me to tell Your Majesty," the valet said as he did so, "that the carriage carrying the Grand Duke is in sight."

"Then I must hurry," the King replied.

As if his words awakened Zita from a dream in which it was hard to think clearly or to understand what was happening, she picked up the King's discarded coffee-cup, put it on the tray, and without saying anything walked towards the door.

She had reached it when the King looked towards her and said almost sharply, as if it was a command:

"Do not forget what I said to you, Zita."

"I will not forget, Your Majesty."

She dropped him a little curtsey, and as she did so she had

no idea how extremely graceful her movement was. Then without looking at him, but aware that he was watching her, she went from the room.

Only as she shut the door behind her was she aware that her heart was beating frantically in her breast and she felt as if she had been swimming in a rough sea.

Although it had been exhilarating, exciting, and dangerous, she felt almost exhausted from the drama of it.

*

Riding home, Zita recalled everything that had happened and could hardly believe the whole thing was not part of her imagination.

She had seen the King, she had talked to him, and, incredibly, he had said he wanted to see her again.

This was something she had not expected, but now she knew he must forget her if only for Sophie's sake.

Then she told herself that whatever the King might suggest to her, it must not encroach in any way on his feelings for Sophie or his courtship, if that was what he intended.

Her status in his eyes would in fact be the same as that occupied by *La Belle* and the other ladies of the *demi-monde* whom he entertained in Paris or in the *Château* that adjoined the Palace in Valdastien.

She thought how horrified her mother would be if she knew not only what she had done but the manner in which the King had looked at her and spoken to her.

'I suppose all men are the same,' Zita thought. 'A pretty face, and they are ready to become familiar, which is something a Princess should not allow.'

At the same time, she thought how very much easier it was to talk to the King as a pretty waitress than it would be at a formal dinner-party.

There they would have Courtiers to the right of them and Courtiers to the left of them and her mother with an eagle-eye watching them from the end of the table.

Then she had the strange feeling that it would be easy to talk to the King in any circumstances; it was not so much what they said but what was left unsaid, and the vibrations which linked them together.

'That is what I felt about him,' Zita thought to herself as she rode back to the Palace. 'I wonder if he felt the same about me.'

There had been no doubt that as his eyes looked into hers it had been impossible for her to look away, and she had felt almost as if he was reaching out towards her, and it was impossible to stop herself from responding.

"He is fascinating, just as I knew he would be," she said aloud.

Pegasus pricked up his ears at the sound of her voice, and she bent forward to pat the horse's neck, saying:

"Yes, he is magnificent, and at the same time unpredictable and of course attracted by any pretty face wherever he finds it."

All the stories she had heard about the King came rushing back to her mind.

There was not only *La Belle;* there were the famous beauties of *le monde* in Paris, as well as the ladies of the *demi-monde,* both of whom *Madame* Goutier had described to her, and the actresses that the Professor had spoken about with a note in his voice which told Zita he was not too old to be attracted by them himself.

'The King is sublimely unconcerned,' she thought, 'whether they are actresses from *Le Théâtre de variétés* or waitresses at The Inn of the Golden Cross.'

She wondered what the King would feel when, having sent her a note as he had said he would, he received a reply from Gretel that Zita was not there.

She thought it would serve him right if she let him wait for her either at the Inn or wherever he told her to come to him in the City.

Then she had thought that was too unkind, so instead she

had told Gretel what was happening and asked her to open any note that was addressed to her.

Gretel listened wide-eyed.

"You have made a conquest of him!" she exclaimed. "But be careful, Princess, or you will be getting yourself into trouble."

"I certainly will if Mama or Papa find out what I have been doing," Zita agreed.

"How are they likely to do that?" Gretel asked. "His Majesty has the reputation of being a Don Juan, but nobody has ever heard of his taking up with the pretty waitress of an Inn before!"

She thought it over before she added:

"You don't look like one, and it's no use pretending you do."

"Then what do I look like?" Zita asked defiantly.

"A Princess!" Gretel retorted, and they both laughed.

At the same time, when Zita reached the Palace and went up the side staircase to the School-Room, she was thinking that if it had been frustrating before not to be allowed to meet the King while he was in the Palace, now it was a thousand times worse.

All she could do was to think of him downstairs, sitting through a dreary, interminable luncheon, with speeches he would doubtless have heard hundreds of times before. If she had been there she would at least have been able to watch him.

Perhaps occasionally their eyes would have met and they would have known what each other was thinking.

She gave a sudden shudder.

'I must be mad,' she thought, 'to imagine he would think of me or that, if I was myself, he would give me a second glance. The only thing that intrigued him about me was the fact that I did not look like the usual Inn-Keeper's daughter, and he was puzzled by the way I could speak three languages.'

Then she remembered what he had said about her hair, and it suddenly struck her that if he saw her grandmother's portrait in the Throne-Room, he might suspect who she was.

But there was no reason why he should, because it was not on the programme for him to go to the Throne-Room, and that was the only place in the Palace where there was a really good portrait of her grandmother.

'This is becoming like a detective-story,' Zita thought, 'where the villain keeps leaving clues behind and sooner or later is bound to be caught!'

She felt herself give a little shiver at the idea of her mother eventually finding out what she had done, and she was quite certain the punishment would inevitably fit the crime.

For the rest of the afternoon she lay on her bed and tried to read a book, but all the time she kept thinking of the King and wondering whether tonight, or perhaps tomorrow, he would send a message to the Inn asking her to meet him.

Just for a moment she played with the fantasy of doing what he asked.

Then she knew that it would not only be far too danger-ous and too complicated, but also from now on she must play fairly and let him concentrate on Sophie.

Once they were engaged, she would have to swear him to secrecy not to reveal to anybody that he had met his sister-in-law in very unusual circumstances.

"I am sure he will be sportsman enough not to give me away," Zita consoled herself, and tried hard to concentrate on her book.

Tonight there was to be the Court Ball, and she felt it was unlikely that the King would think there was any chance for him to see her at the Inn or anywhere else, and he would be obliged to dance in the flower-filled Ball-Room downstairs until at least one o'clock in the morning.

That was the usual time, she had learnt from the Lord

Chamberlain, that her mother liked her parties to end, and when the National Anthem had been played there would be nothing else the guests could do but go home.

A rather unappetising dinner was brought upstairs to Zita.

Baroness Mekszath, who was very much under the Grand Duchess's thumb, looked in twice during the day to see if Zita was all right.

When Zita said she was, she hurried away thankfully to return to the festivities downstairs.

Her last visit was just before dinner, and she came into Zita's room in her best evening-gown, a small tiara on her greying hair and a look of excitement on her face, which was unusual.

"What is happening?" Zita enquired.

"Oh, it is all very thrilling, Your Royal Highness!" the Baroness replied. "His Majesty is the most handsome man you have ever seen."

"What does Sophie think of him?"

The Baroness hesitated for a moment before she answered:

"I think Her Royal Highness is a little shy. She sat next to him at luncheon, but they did not seem to have much to say to each other, and I thought His Majesty was somewhat preoccupied."

"In what way?"

The Baroness found it difficult to reply.

"To tell the truth, His Majesty did not seem to be making much effort," she said. "My mother always said that whatever company you find yourself in . . . "

The Baroness was off on another of the rambling stories of her youth, but Zita was not listening.

She was thinking that if she had been at the luncheon she would have found a great deal to say to the King, the most important thing being his attitude towards Germany.

After that she could think of nothing more interesting

than to talk to him about his horses and compare them with the ones he would see in Aldross.

It was obvious that the Baroness had no wish to stay upstairs when she might be enjoying herself below, and she soon left Zita, advising her to go to bed early.

'I do not have much choice!' Zita thought drily.

She refused the last course the footmen brought her, and walking petulantly across her room she wondered what would happen if she went downstairs to peep through the Ball-Room window.

She knew that if she did so and was seen, her mother would be furiously angry.

She then played with the idea of putting on her best gown, which was green, to match her eyes, and walking into the Ball-Room to say that after all she had decided to join the party.

She could imagine the consternation this would cause and the anger in her mother's eyes and the hatred in Sophie's.

"Even Papa would look at me with disgust," Zita told herself, and decided again that it would be an unsporting thing to do.

For if the King did not propose to Sophie, Zita would be reproached over and over again for all eternity for having prevented him from doing so.

Finally, when she had flung the novel she was reading across the room because it was so boring, she got into bed and extinguished the candles.

Far away in the distance she thought she could hear the sound of music, and because she could not close her ears to it, she pretended she was waltzing with the King.

As he held her in his arms, she could feel them vibrating to each other so that the music came not only from the violins but from their hearts.

Chapter Four

IT WAS impossible to sleep, and after a while Zita drew back the curtains from her bedroom window and looked up at the stars, wondering what fate and the future held for her.

She knew that because of her position in life, however much she fought against it, sooner or later she would have to accept a marriage which was advantageous to her country or politically expedient in one way or another.

Ever since she was a child she had had it drummed into her that being Royal had great responsibilities.

She knew now that what her mother had really been saying to her was that as a Royal Princess her only service was to make a marriage which would in some way be an advantage to Aldross.

Therefore, when she had imagined love and dreamt of it, Zita had seen herself not as a Princess but as an ordinary girl, as she was unable to be in real life.

The man of her dreams was faceless and not of Royal birth.

She had told herself stories in which the man she loved was Hungarian, a magnificent rider, a man with whom she danced wildly to gypsy music, or galloped over the Steppes side by side with him into an indefinable horizon.

Alternatively, she would imagine she fell in love with an Englishman who owned fine horses. They would watch them win the Derby or the Gold Cup at Ascot, and, walking beside him, she would lead their horse into the unsaddling enclosure.

Both her father and her mother had told her what happened at race-meetings in England and how their organisation and setting were superior to those in any other country in the world.

She had also imagined a large, impressive Georgian mansion which her husband would own, and they would live there quietly, training their horses and playing only a very small part in the affairs of the country.

This was the life her mother had lived as an obscure member of Queen Victoria's family, until it had been decided that she would marry the Grand Duke of Aldross.

"Tell me more about your childhood, Mama," Zita would plead.

When she was young, the Grand Duchess had talked both to her and to Sophie in a human and revealing manner.

It was only when Zita grew so pretty that her mother pushed her aside and kept her confidential reminiscences for her favourite, elder daughter.

There was one nationality that never figured in Zita's dreams, and that was the French.

Although she was fascinated by the descriptions of the beauty of Paris and its gaiety and extravagant glamour, she had learnt from *Madame* Goutier that nearly all Frenchmen had arranged marriages.

These were socially advantageous to their families, and a wife's dowry was of tremendous importance, but also married men regularly had mistresses, who were kept entirely apart from their family life.

At the same time, such women were considered of equal importance in contributing to a man's happiness.

'I would hate that!' Zita thought.

It flashed through her mind that Sophie would find it humiliating if she ever learnt that the King, like so many Frenchmen, had a wife in public and a mistress in private.

'Perhaps Sophie, because she is rather stupid, will never find out,' Zita thought consolingly.

At the same time, she felt what was almost a disgust at the idea of the King, or any other man, leading a double life.

Now her thoughts were of her father and mother, and she knew, although it might be wrong of her, that her sympathy was entirely with her father.

'Mama is so cold, and Papa likes warm, laughing, extrovered women,' she thought.

She tried to imagine her father kissing her mother passionately and found it impossible. In fact she could not think of her mother as passionate in any way, except with anger.

Even then, because she was English, the Grand Duchess had an almost inviolate control over her feelings.

When she was really incensed with one of her daughters or anybody else, she only grew stiff until she appeared to be made of marble, and her voice was cold like the ice that covered the lakes in winter.

She was very unlike the people of Aldross, who, if they were angry, raged, screamed, and threw things at one another!

The next moment they would put out their arms and, with tears of contrition in their eyes, kiss passionately and insistently to wipe away any unhappiness they might have caused.

'I am sure life is much easier like that,' Zita thought.

She remembered how often she had been punished as a child for losing her temper or for saying what she thought.

"Royalty do not show emotion," the Grand Duchess had said over and over again. "Royalty do not cry in public—Royalty hide their feelings behind a mask."

"Why? Why? Why?" Zita had enquired, until she was smacked into not arguing with her mother or with her Governesses, who voiced much the same admonishments.

Once she had stamped her foot and cried:

"I hate being a Royal Princess! I am going to run away and live with the gypsies and you will never see me again!"

She had run from the room and had even got as far as leaving the Palace, determined never to return.

But she had been brought back, smacked, and sent to

bed for the rest of the day with only bread and water for supper.

She did not feel repentent, but she had learnt that it was more prudent not to express her feelings so volubly but to keep them to herself.

All these thoughts brought her back to the King, and she told herself that although it was very exciting to talk to him, and it would be even more thrilling to flirt with him, she was very sorry for Sophie.

'If she falls in love with him as Mama did with Papa,' Zita thought, 'she will sit in the Palace with an aching heart while the King is visiting *La Belle* or somebody like her, or having a very important "diplomatic engagement" in Paris.'

She wanted to laugh at the idea, then insidiously, almost as if somebody were whispering in her ear, she thought that whatever the suffering afterwards, it might be worthwhile for Sophie if she was made love to by the King rather than the stolid Margrave of Baden-Baden.

Zita looked up at the sky and realised she had been thinking for so long that the stars were not now as bright as they had been.

Because dawn came earlier at this time of the year, very soon there would be the first glow of it on the other side of the mountains.

She decided she would ride as she had yesterday morning, but today there was no hurry because everybody in the Palace would be exhausted after the Ball last night.

She dressed slowly, putting on the full skirt of a green riding-habit which was light and very becoming for the summer, and wearing with it a thin muslin blouse inset with bands of lace and a jacket to match.

It made Zita look very fresh and young, and because she had no intention of wearing a riding-hat since no-one would see her, she merely brushed her long red hair until it seemed to dance as if it had a life of its own.

She then tied it at the base of her neck with a green satin ribbon.

By the time she was ready, a glow was rising in the sky and turning the snow on the peaks to gold.

Zita walked through the Palace by the same route that she had the day before, unbolted the side door which was the nearest she could get to the stables, and went outside.

She noticed that since the King had arrived the number of sentries had been increased, and when she had saddled Pegasus she realised that it would be impossible to leave the Palace grounds by any of the main gates.

She therefore guided him through the trees until in front of them was a five-barred gate which was the entrance used by the gardeners.

There were no sentries on duty there, and while the gate was padlocked, it did not constitute a serious obstacle for Pegasus. He jumped the gate with ease and with a good six inches to spare.

Then they were trotting down back lanes and uninhabited ways towards the meadowlands which Zita was sure were very like the Steppes of Hungary, which she had always longed to see.

By the time she reached the valley, the mist which hung over it early in the morning was just beginning to rise, and she felt as if she were riding into a mythical world of dreams which had nothing to do with the Palace and the world she had left behind her.

Because she had so much time on her hands she took Pegasus gently through the mist until it began to vanish altogether and now she could see the brilliance of the flowers.

As the first rays of the sun came over the peaks, they filled the whole valley with a golden glow.

It was so beautiful that it made Zita wish she could show it to the King and challenge him to produce anything so lovely in his own country.

Then as she thought of him lying asleep in the Palace, some instinct made her look back over her shoulder and she saw in the distance a man riding towards her.

She stopped and thought with a sudden sense of apprehension that she had been seen leaving the stables and somebody had been sent to bring her back.

Then as the rider came a little nearer she had an idea that seemed completely incredible, and yet with every stride of his horse towards her she became convinced that it was in fact the King.

For some reason which she could not explain to herself, she waited for him.

Then when she saw that her supposition was true and it was the King riding a huge black stallion not unlike Pegasus, a sudden gleam of mischief came into her green eyes.

She knew he had seen her, knew he was spurring his horse in order to catch up with her, and she waited just a few seconds longer before she touched Pegasus with her whip and started him off at a gallop.

She knew it was what Pegasus had been wanting ever since they had come from the Palace, and he moved so swiftly that it seemed as if his hoofs scarcely touched the ground.

Zita knew that this was a challenge that no rider like the King could resist.

Without looking back, she was aware that he was galloping too . . . striving by every means in his power to catch up with her.

She was determined that he should not do so, and yet she could hear his stallion coming nearer and nearer until finally they were galloping side by side at a speed that Zita knew she had never reached before in all her years on horseback.

They rode for a long way and as she glanced at him Zita was aware that he rode better than any other man she had ever seen, and that included her father, who was exceptional.

The King seemed part of his horse, and she knew that just as his stallion was magnificent, so was he.

They rode until the speed of their gallop seemed to snatch the breath from their lips.

Then as if they communicated without words and knew they had done enough, they gradually reined in their two horses, who were as breathless as their riders.

Zita turned a laughing face to the King.

"A dead heat, I think, Your Majesty! Or must I, as a woman, concede to you the victory?"

"I will accept that we are both the victors," the King replied, "but I would like to know how it is possible that a mere woman can ride so well."

Zita laughed and the sound seemed to ring out in the quiet of the morning.

The King pulled his stallion to a halt before he said:

"Your horse is superb. To whom does he belong?"

"He is mine," Zita replied, "and as you can imagine, I love him very much."

"As doubtless you love the person who gave him to you."

There was a note in the King's voice that she found jarring.

She looked at him for an explanation and he said:

"As the gentleman in question is obviously wealthy, it seems extraordinary that he should allow you to work at an Inn."

Zita smiled, wondering what she should reply, and the King asked harshly:

"What does this man mean to you? Do you love him as you love his horse?"

Zita was so astonished at the question that for a moment she only looked at the King in a bewildered fashion before she understood exactly what he was implying.

Then as she was aware that what he was saying classed her with *La Belle* and the other women with whom he was rumoured to associate, her chin went up defiantly.

"As I consider what you have said offensive, Your Majesty," she said coldly, "I will leave you."

She would have turned Pegasus round, but as she did so the King with a swift movement bent forward to catch hold of his bridle.

Surprised, the horse reared, but the King did not relinquish his hold. He only said:

"You cannot leave me. I want to talk to you."

"I am not certain that I wish to talk to Your Majesty!"

Then as Zita spoke her eyes met his and she knew it would be impossible for her to leave.

They looked at each other. Then as if she compelled him to do so, the King said quietly:

"Forgive me, but you must be aware that everything you say and do puzzles and perplexes me. In fact, unless you can give me an explanation and answer my questions, I think I shall go mad!"

Because he spoke seriously, Zita felt shy and looked away from him before she said:

"I cannot imagine why Your Majesty should . . . concern himself about me."

The King released Pegasus and said:

"That is the only foolish remark you have made since we first met. Let us continue our ride."

Zita turned Pegasus round and they moved side by side into the sunshine.

The mist had now fully cleared from the lower part of the valley, but it still hung over the trees which the sun had not yet reached and obscured the Palace in the distance so that it seemed as if they were in an enchanted land of their own.

They rode on and the only sound was the tinkle of harness. Zita, aware that the King was looking at her searchingly, penetratingly, was glad that he was puzzled and thought it right that everything was not so straightforward and simple that he knew before she spoke what she was about to say.

"I am waiting," the King remarked after a little while.

"For what?"

"To hear what you have to tell me."

"Why should I tell you anything?" Zita asked. "Is it not more amusing to know that we have met, perhaps through the manipulations of fate? As in a dream, there is no need for explanations, or for everything about it to have a reason."

She spoke as she might have done to her father, and when the King did not answer she went on:

"Dreams are lovely only if one does not wake up and try to make them come true."

"Are you seriously suggesting," the King asked, "that when you leave me this morning I shall know no more about you than I do at this moment?"

"Why not?" Zita enquired. "I did not mean to meet you here."

"Fate brought us together again," the King said. "That and the fact that I could not sleep for thinking of you."

Zita looked at him sharply.

It seemed strange that he should say that when she too had been unable to sleep for thinking of him.

"Now Your Majesty is exaggerating," she said. "If you did not sleep it was doubtless because of the food you ate at supper or perhaps you imbibed too much champagne."

"That sounds very plausible," the King replied, "but you know as well as I do that it is not true, and I am not speaking lightly. Ever since I saw you yesterday at the Inn, Zita, I have wanted you."

"How strange!" Zita murmured, and nearly added that she had wanted him.

The King was about to say something more when a butterfly fluttering at his stallion's feet flew up and brushed the animal's nose so that he shied.

The King quickly brought him under control, then said:

"I must talk to you! Let us find somewhere where we can sit instead of riding."

As he spoke he glanced towards the woods.

"About a mile ahead," Zita replied, "there is a small Inn used by those who climb the mountain above it. I am sure they can supply us with coffee, if you have not yet had your breakfast."

The King smiled.

"To be honest, I sneaked out without disturbing anybody. I thought it might cause a commotion if I demanded one of my horses so early, and I was quite certain they would think it strange that I should want to ride alone."

Knowing exactly what he was saying and that a very early order would disturb the servants in the Palace besides the grooms in the stables, Zita gave a little laugh.

But she knew she must not show that she understood.

Instead, she touched Pegasus to make him move quicker, the King followed, and they rode on in silence.

The Inn was one that Zita had visited last when she was with her father on one of their climbing trips.

She thought it was unlikely that the same people would be in charge, but even if they were strangers they might know who she was since everybody in Aldross knew the family of their Ruler.

The Inn was a small chalet surrounded by trees which had been built a little way up the side of the mountain, but not high enough for the horses to have any difficulty in reaching it.

As Zita had expected, there were tables and chairs in front of it, some of them enclosed in little vine-covered arbours so that anyone wanting to talk intimately could be almost isolated from the other guests.

It was so early in the morning that there was nobody at the tables ordering either the thin light wine that grew in this part of the valley, or the beer that came from the Capital, which was therefore more expensive.

"Shall I put your horse in the stable?" the King asked as they dismounted.

"Pegasus will be quite all right. He will not wander far and will come when I call him."

"So Pegasus is his name," the King remarked. "I would not be surprised if he grew wings and you flew away on him."

"I promise not to do that until I have had my coffee," Zita answered.

She knotted the reins on Pegasus's neck and set him free. Then after a moment's hesitation, as if he could not concede that Zita could control her horse better than he could, the King did the same.

"I think, as it is so early, you will have to go into the house to order the coffee," Zita said. "I imagine they will not be expecting customers until the sun is fully risen."

As she spoke she thought that perhaps as he imagined her to be a waitress the King would expect her to perform such a task. But for the moment, she argued with herself, they were on equal terms.

Without waiting for his reply, she walked towards the nearest little arbour which was covered with vine-leaves and bunches of grapes just beginning to ripen.

Zita sat down in the most inconspicuous seat and hoped that when the coffee came the person carrying it would not look too closely at her.

The King was away for some time and in fact she was surprised that he should be so long.

When he did reappear he was followed by a large, fat, elderly woman carrying a tray and a table-cloth. She plonked them both down on the table, saying as she did so:

"You must arrange them yourself, *Mein Herr,* otherside my croissants will burn. I can't leave them any longer."

"We can manage," the King replied, and without even a glance at Zita the fat woman hurried away.

The King lifted the tray as Zita spread the red and white checked tablecloth over the iron table, and then set it down in front of her.

It contained a large pot of coffee, two cups, a small bowl filled with thick cream, and a basket in which was a selection of fruit.

"You were a long time," she said. "I wondered what had happened."

"The croissants were more important than I," the King replied.

Zita laughed.

"I know why you are laughing," he said.

"But of course!" Zita answered. "I was thinking how very chastening it was for His Majesty King Maximilian of Valdastien to find there was an occasion in his life when he took second place to a croissant!"

"I am prepared to admit it is something that has not happened before."

She passed him his cup filled with coffee, and he added as he took it from her:

"And this is also the first time I have ever been with anybody quite as beautiful as you!"

"You say that too glibly!" Zita replied. "I realise you have had a lot of practice. At the same time, any producer of a Play would make you repeat and repeat it until it sounded really credible."

"So you *are* an actress!" the King said. "I told myself that your performance yesterday was too real to be true."

Zita laughed.

"If that is what you want to believe, then you must believe it!"

"I want you to tell me the truth."

"How disappointing it would be if after all you have imagined, I turn out to be just the daughter of a cobbler!"

"I doubt if a cobbler's daughter would look as you do and would ride a mythical animal called Pegasus as if she too came from Olympus."

"That is very poetical," Zita teased.

"You are beginning to annoy me," the King said. "Let us stop pretending and talk sensibly."

"I am sorry to disappoint you, but this is how I always talk, when I get the chance."

"You do not disappoint me," the King replied, "you speak in the same way as you look, as if you had stepped from a dream. I am only terrified that I may wake up."

"That is something you must not do," Zita said quickly, "so stop prodding and pinching yourself to see if you are asleep! If you do, you will suddenly open your eyes and find yourself in your own bed and . . . alone."

She said the last word without thinking about it, and only as she saw the expression in the King's eyes did she realise that he had interpreted it very differently.

"What do you mean by that?" he asked. "What do you know about me apart from the fact that I am a Royal Visitor to your Capital?"

He spoke crossly, and because she could not help it, Zita laughed.

"Do you imagine that is all anybody knows about Your Majesty? Because you are our next-door neighbour, we have been talking about the love-affairs of King Maximilian ever since I can remember."

"And what did you hear about them?" the King enquired.

Zita wondered if she should tell him the truth.

She could hear *Madame* Goutier reading letters from her daughter about his exploits in Paris; the Professor describing the charms of actresses at *Le Théâtre de Variétés* and the singers who had taken the City by storm at the Café-Concerts.

Her thoughts brought her back to *La Belle,* who was the guest of the King in the *Château* next to the Palace in Valdastien.

As she was thinking what she should say, the King was watching the expression in her eyes and he said suddenly:

"Who could have told you such things, and why are you so ready to believe them?"

Zita turned her face away from him.

"You are . . . not to read my . . . thoughts."

"Why not?" the King asked. "And may I say that because I

think I can read them, it is the strangest, most unaccountable thing that could possibly have happened to me."

Zita looked at him as if she could not help it.

As her eyes met his she knew that what he said was true.

In some strange, unaccountable way, he knew what she was thinking, while at the same time she could read his thoughts and knew that he was not only interested but intrigued and almost mesmerised by her.

He had in fact lain awake thinking of her, and he had felt that the only way to escape from those thoughts, which were so strange, so insistent, and so uncomfortable, was to ride.

They looked at each other for a long time until the King said:

"Why has this happened to you and me, Zita?"

Because she felt a little frightened she replied:

"I . . . I am not admitting that . . . it has."

"Not in words, perhaps," the King said in a low voice, "but just as I know what you are thinking, so I can feel you vibrating to me as I am vibrating to you."

Zita drew in her breath.

"You are not to say . . . that! It is not . . . true!"

The King smiled.

"Why lie about anything that is so enchanting?" he asked. "I felt frightened last night in case I never saw you again. Now I know I need not have worried. We have been drawn to each other in the same way as the moon draws the tides."

Zita drew in her breath. Then she said:

"That is a very good simile. The moon is far away in the Heavens, and although it may have an effect on the sea, there is no question of the moon and the sea, any more than of us, ever coming closer to each other."

The King suddenly brought his clenched fist down on the table with a sound that made Zita jump and the cups and saucers rattle.

"Nonsense!" he exclaimed. "We have to see each other! And that is what I intend to talk to you about."

"It is . . . impossible!"

"Why?"

"Because as I said, you are as far away as the Man in the Moon, who does not come down to earth to consort with human beings like myself."

"I am a human being," the King objected, "and if necessary I am quite certain Pegasus would be able to fly you to the moon."

Zita laughed because it was a reply she had not expected.

"I wish Pegasus could understand how flattering you are being to him."

"Now we are back to Pegasus," the King said, "and I am still waiting to hear who gave him to you."

Zita did not answer, and the King said:

"You were angry when I made the obvious suggestion, but you cannot be so cruel as to leave me wondering and tortured by an emotion I have never felt before."

Because she could not help it, Zita looked at him questioningly, and the King said suddenly:

"Very well, I am jealous as I can never remember being in the past. Who is he?"

"I do not think Your Majesty has any right to ask me that . . . sort of question."

"Then give me the right."

"I . . . do not know . . . what you mean."

"I think you do, but I am afraid to put it into words."

She knew then that he was offering her the place in his life already occupied by *La Belle*.

While she knew she should be shocked by the suggestion and very angry, she could only sit wondering frantically what she could say without immediately quarrelling about it to the point where they could not go on talking to each other.

Because she knew that to talk to him was what she wanted to do, because to be with the King was the most intriguing, exciting thing that had ever happened to her in her whole life, she could not suddenly end it like the letting down of the curtain at the end of a Play.

The King was watching her face and she knew he was trying to read her thoughts.

Then he said unexpectedly:

"I do not believe you can look like you do and not be pure. Has any man possessed you?"

Because Zita had never in her wildest dreams ever imagined any man would ask her anything so intimate or so impertinent, for a moment her eyes only widened as she looked at him incredulously.

Then the colour flooded into her cheeks and she replied without thinking:

"Of course . . . not! How could you . . . think such a . . . thing?"

The King made an exclamation of triumph and put his hand over hers as he said:

"I knew it! Forgive me, but after you told me you had been given Pegasus as a present, I felt as if all the devils of hell were taunting me."

"I do not want to . . . discuss myself, nor should you . . . talk to me in such a way," Zita said hesitatingly.

She knew it was a weak reply, but because the King's hand was still touching hers she felt as if the vibrations of which he had spoken were pulsating from him to her and she could feel them running up her arms and into her breasts almost like little shafts of sunshine.

"You are so beautiful!" the King said in a low voice. "So absurdly, ridiculously beautiful! I have always believed there was somebody in the world who would look like my mother, but I expected if I ever found her it would be in Hungary."

"Then why have you not . . . looked for her . . . there?" Zita managed to ask.

The King gave a sigh.

"For several reasons," he said. "Firstly, I have no wish to

marry; secondly, I never thought the Hungarian temperament—impetuous, impulsive, wild, and emotional—would fit in with my wife as Ruler of Valdastien."

Zita understood exactly what he was saying.

Although her grandmother and grandfather had been ideally happy as man and wife, she had known that as Grand Duchess of Aldross her grandmother had often scandalised and shocked the more staid citizens of her new country.

When she and her husband had quarrelled, the whole Palace had vibrated with the violence of it. When they had made up, however, everything had been enveloped, as one romantic old Courtier had told her, "in sunshine."

Aloud Zita said:

"There is a proverb in my country which says: 'It is better to live than to exist,' and another: 'It is better to be too warm by the fire than to freeze in the snow.' "

The King put back his head and laughed.

"How can you be not only beautiful but also intelligent and witty? Every moment I am with you, Zita, I become more and more convinced that I am in fact asleep and dreaming."

"Then do not try to wake up."

She would have taken her hand from his, but he held on to it.

"I am not going to lose you," he said, "until you promise that because we are both dreaming here together we can go on doing so in the future."

His eyes searched her face as he said:

"We both know that what has happened since we met is not just exceptional but unique. We have found each other across time and space. If we lost each other again, it would be a crime for which we would never forgive ourselves."

"It is something we . . . have to do," Zita said softly. "You have your life to lead . . . and I have . . . mine."

"What is your life? That is what I am trying to persuade you to tell me," the King said.

She did not answer and he went on:

"Whatever you are doing now, why should your future not be with me? I want you, Zita, I want you as a woman, and also I want you to help me, to inspire me, in ways which I have never thought of until now."

He looked away from her as he said:

"I know intuitively that they are like doors opening onto new projects and new interests which will help not only me but the people over whom I rule."

He suddenly took his hand from Zita's and put it up to his forehead.

"I cannot think why I am saying this to you, but it seems to come to my lips without my brain or my will controlling it, and yet strangely and inexplicably I know it is true."

"You are . . . frightening me," Zita said. "How can you really think such things when we have . . . only just . . . met?"

"Now you are stepping outside our dream," the King said. "We have met twice, but I have been looking for you, trying to find you again, through hundreds of different lives."

"Do you really believe that?"

She put her elbows on the table and cupped her face with her hands.

"I have tried to puzzle out for myself the doctrine of reincarnation, but I have never had anybody to whom I could talk about it."

The King smiled.

"It is a very large subject, and yet to one who has been to the East it seems entirely understandable as the only real justice."

He paused before he went on:

"But at the moment I am not concerned with reincarnation, either as a faith or as an argument. I am concerned with you and me, Zita, and that is the problem we have to decide—and quickly."

"How can we decide anything in such a hurry?"

"I am leaving Aldross tomorrow," the King said, "and tonight the Grand Duke has arranged a meeting with the Prime Minister and Members of the Cabinet in which we will discuss our position with regard to Germany."

As he spoke Zita knew that if her father had arranged that meeting he must hope that he would be able to announce that the King in marrying Sophie would unite their two countries and therefore strengthen their resistance to a German Federation.

Then almost as if the words came to her lips without her conscious volition she asked:

"Are you ... intending to ... marry the ... Princess Sophie?"

Chapter Five

THERE was a pause before the King asked:

"Is that what the people of Aldross are expecting?"

"Of course they are," Zita replied.

"Why?"

"You know the answer to that. I cannot believe that you, of all people, are not aware of Bismarck's ambitions and the greed of Prussia."

The King raised his eye-brows.

She knew he was extremely surprised that she should be aware of the political aspect of his visit.

He hesitated as if he would be evasive in his reply. Then he said:

"Actually I have decided that tonight, when I meet your Prime Minister and Statesmen, I will put forward a proposition for a closer commercial relationship between our two countries, which would also involve defence."

Zita gave a little exclamation of pleasure and the King went on:

"I cannot think why it should not be extended to other Monarchies and Principalities also in this part of Europe."

Now she gave a cry which seemed to ring out round the small arbour.

"You mean we should have a Federation too? How clever of you! Why did . . . nobody else . . . think of that?"

As she spoke she thought that her father and the Prime Minister had been extremely obtuse in not putting such an idea into operation before now.

"It certainly seems to be reasonable, as we have so much in common," the King said quietly.

Zita's eyes were shining as she said again:

"It is very . . . very . . . clever of you to have thought of it! I am sure that those who have been worrying about the grandiose ambitions of Prussia will be very grateful."

The King leant back in his chair as if to look at her more easily in another perspective.

"How can you possibly know so much or be so interested in such things?" he asked.

Zita laughed.

"Now you are being rude! What you are really saying is that a woman should confine her interests to her home, her husband, and her children."

"As you do not possess the last two," the King said, "I should have thought you might be completely preoccupied by your dancing, and of course your face."

"I still have a brain in my head."

"I am aware of that, and I am therefore glad that you approve of my plan."

"I not only approve of it, but I know that the Grand Duke and those who rule over my country will be delighted."

As she spoke it struck Zita that if this was the King's way of avoiding an obligation to marry Sophie, her mother would be extremely disappointed.

What she was thinking must have shown in her eyes, because the King said quietly:

"I think you have found a snag. What is it?"

Quickly, because she was afraid of the way he could read her thoughts, Zita answered:

"I was thinking that in our Federation—and you must find another name for it since I could not bear to copy the Prussians—you must not include or go too near Bulgaria."

"Why do you say that?" the King asked sharply.

"Because a revolution is being planned to liberate the country!"

The King stared at Zita as if he found her answer incredible.

"How can you know that?"

Zita could have replied very easily that one of her relatives had told them that underground organisations in Rumania were in touch with revolutionaries in Bulgaria.

But this was not public knowledge and she therefore said lightly:

"It is only something I have heard."

The King bent forward with his elbows on the table.

"You are making it even more difficult for me, Zita."

"In what way?"

"You have to tell me how it is that you know what no young woman in the position in which I saw you yesterday could possibly know, and how you can sit here talking to me on equal terms."

Zita gave a little laugh.

"If that is true, Your Majesty, I am very . . . flattered."

"Now you are not being natural but are acting a part," the King said sharply, "and I am determined to know the truth."

"I have already begged you to leave things as they are. This is a dream we are dreaming together, and if you step out of it, you will be disillusioned or disappointed, and that would be a mistake."

"You surprise me," the King said, "as you have done since I first saw you standing with the sunshine on your hair. And my instinct tells me that I shall not be disillusioned, however long we know each other."

"Your Majesty has already said you are leaving tomorrow, and that does not give you much time in which to lose your illusions."

The King looked away from her and she knew he was considering what he should say.

Because she thought it was a mistake to hurry him, she picked a greengage out of the basket of fruit and ate it, thinking as she did so that they should return soon to the City.

It would be a great mistake if it was discovered in the Palace that they were both unaccountably missing.

It was unlikely that anybody who learnt that both she and the King had gone riding very early would suppose that they were together, but Zita had found in the past that there were always eyes and ears in the Palace where one least expected them.

And there were lips, too, that were only too ready to repeat to her mother anything that was the least out of the ordinary.

It seemed as if the King suddenly made up his mind and he said:

"As I have already told you, Zita, I am leaving Aldross tomorrow, and I had intended to go next to Bosnia. But I have changed my mind."

"It would naturally be the next country to join your anti-Prussian line of defence."

"I know," the King replied, "but Bosnia will have to wait. I intend to go first to a Castle I own in the mountains about twenty miles from here."

"I know what you are talking about!" Zita exclaimed. "The Castle of Kovac!"

"You have heard of it?"

"I have heard that it is very impressive and was once used by the Kings of Valdastien as an impregnable Fort of Defence against the aggressive warriors of Aldross."

The King laughed.

"I had forgotten that. There are no warring warriors there today, but the views over my country are breathtakingly lovely and something I want you to see."

As he finished speaking he looked deep into Zita's eyes, and as the full impact of what he had said percolated into her mind, she thought her heart stopped beating.

Then as she stared at him, finding it hard to believe that he was actually inviting her to go there with him, the King put his hand over hers.

"We could be very happy, Zita, in my Castle in the clouds," he said softly. "I have only just realised that when I have been there in the past I have always been alone, and that was because it was you who were missing."

Zita could feel the vibrations emanating from him and she thought perhaps he could feel hers.

Then she said, and her voice was low and almost incoherent:

"Is Your Majesty . . . suggesting something . . . which I know is not only . . . wrong, but very . . . very . . . insulting?"

The King's fingers tightened on hers sharply.

"You know I do not mean it to be that," he said. "But I want you with me, I want to talk to you, to listen to you, and above all to make love to you."

Now Zita stiffened, and she would have taken her hand from his if he had not prevented her from doing so.

"I think Your Majesty is aware," she said after a moment, "that such a . . . suggestion is not only . . . something to which I could never in any . . . circumstances agree . . . but is also very . . . wrong from your point of view at this . . . particular moment."

The King looked surprised and Zita went on:

"You came here yesterday and were seen off by your Statesmen on a mission of goodwill which concerned Valdastien as much as Aldross. Now the least you can do, if you believe your mission has been completed, is to inform them what has been arranged."

She paused, then went on firmly:

"You should also tell them of your new idea of extending the unification of the countries in this area to Bosnia and Serbia, as well as a number of small Principalities which you know will be as vitally concerned as we are."

As Zita finished speaking she realised that the King was looking at her as if he could hardly credit what she was saying, and almost before she had said the last word he remarked sharply:

"Am I to believe you are taking me to task for negligence?"

"No, for indifference," Zita replied without thinking. "If you are truthful, you will admit that you are putting your own interests before those of your country and mine."

She saw the astonishment in the King's eyes.

Then, as if she knew there was nothing more to be said, she rose to her feet.

"If Your Majesty will pay for our coffee," she said, "I will collect the horses."

She did not wait for his answer but walked from the arbour and out of the garden in front of the Inn to where the horses were peacefully cropping the grass under the trees.

She whistled and Pegasus lifted his head and came trotting towards her as she expected.

After a little hesitation the stallion followed.

Before the King came from the Inn, Zita was mounted on Pegasus and held his horse by the reins.

She deliberately had not waited for the King to help her into the saddle because she did not wish him to touch her.

She knew he was astounded at the way she had spoken to him and she suspected that he was also annoyed.

But she had the uncomfortable feeling that if he was very close to her, she might find it hard not to apologise for what she had said, and perhaps by doing so encourage him to say more about their going together to his Castle in the clouds.

'How dare he suggest such a thing!' Zita thought to herself.

But her indignation was false.

She knew it was her own fault that his attitude towards her was the same as it had been to dozens of other women whom he pursued in Paris or brought, like *La Belle*, to the *Château* in Valdastien.

She told herself despairingly that he had spoilt for her

what had been the most exciting and intriguing encounter she had ever imagined in her fantasy-world.

She had wanted to keep it apart forever from the reality of the dull, restricted life she led as a Princess.

Yet her brain forced her to be honest enough to admit that she had invited everything that had happened, first by pretending to be a waitress at The Inn of the Golden Cross, and secondly, although it was by chance that she had met the King this morning, while she had not meant to flirt with him she had certainly behaved in an intimate and provocative manner.

Her mother would have considered it reprehensible if they had been conversing with each other even in one of the Salons in the Palace.

"He assumed I was under the protection of a man like himself who had given me Pegasus," Zita argued to herself, "and although I denied it, I think the idea is still rankling at the back of his mind and he will find it hard to understand that I am not prepared to accept everything he offers on a much larger scale."

The door of the Inn opened and the King came out and as he walked down the steps into the garden she thought that it was difficult to imagine that any man could look more majestic.

'He is every inch a King!' Zita thought to herself.

However, it was extremely deflating that one thing was quite obvious—that she did not look Royal, and the King did not even think of her as an aristocrat.

"There is no reason why he should," she murmured to herself.

At the same time, it was demoralising to know that one had to be labelled to show one's identity rather than that a man should know instinctively that she was not only pure but also too respectable to accept what he proposed.

The King joined her, took his horse's reins in his hand, and sprang into the saddle.

As soon as she released his horse Zita rode ahead without waiting down the twisting path which led towards the valley.

The King followed, and it was impossible for them to speak until they were clear of the trees and in the meadowland.

Then as he rode alongside her she touched Pegasus with her whip and he immediately set off at a gallop, delighted to stretch his legs and knowing that his head was turned in the direction of home.

There was nothing the King could do but gallop too, and they rode very swiftly until Zita pulled in her reins, knowing that Pegasus had had enough, and the towers and spires of the Capital could be seen in the distance and so could the Palace outside the City.

It looked impressive and rather beautiful in the sunshine.

But Zita felt it was a prison waiting for her and once she had returned to her cell she would never be able to escape again.

She drew Pegasus to a standstill.

"I think, Your Majesty," she said, "we must part here and certainly not ride back together."

"Are you thinking of your reputation or of mine?" the King asked mockingly.

"Both!" Zita flashed.

"I can see that what you are saying is sensible," he agreed, "but at the same time, I have no intention of allowing you to leave me until you say when we can meet again."

"There is no point in our doing so."

"That is your opinion."

As she did not answer, he added:

"Have I shocked you by what I have suggested?"

"You know you have!"

"Forgive me," he said in a different tone from what she had expected. "I want so desperately to be with you, I want to talk to you, and even if you will not allow me to make love to you, I still want us to be together."

"That is something we cannot be," Zita answered, "and when we now say good-bye, we will not see each other again."

"Why," the King enquired, "should you wish to shut me out without explanation, without telling me why, if in no other way, I cannot meet you as a citizen of this delightful country?"

"That is a question I am unable to answer," Zita replied, "and there is no point in trying to do so."

She paused before she added:

"It has been very exciting and very . . . very . . . interesting for me to know you, but there is no . . . future in dreams . . . and that is why when you . . . leave Aldross tomorrow we shall not . . . meet again."

As she spoke she was quite certain, without his telling her, that he had no intention of marrying Sophie, and that he had thought up the link between Valdastien and other countries as a way of avoiding matrimony with a Princess from Aldross.

The King's eyes were on her face and after a moment he said, and she was surprised to hear a note of despair in his voice:

"What can I say to you? How can I make you understand how much I want to see you, Zita? Now that we have found each other, I cannot lose you."

"It is something which has to happen."

"But why? Why?"

She looked at the sun rising over the far-away peaks and said:

"I suppose we could stay here all day arguing with each other, and in a way it would be exciting. But there are people waiting for you, and people waiting for me, and it would be a great mistake for any of them to be curious as to where we have been."

"Very well," the King said. "I will leave you if you promise you will meet me here tomorrow morning at the same time. I shall not be expected to leave the Palace until ten o'clock, so I shall be here soon after five."

"If I come, what shall we talk about?"

The King laughed.

"What you are asking in a somewhat indirect manner is whether I shall try to persuade you to leave with me when I say good-bye to the Grand Duke at The Inn of the Golden Cross."

Zita did not reply and after a moment he said:

"If I swear to you to talk of everything else but that, will you come tomorrow morning?"

It flashed through Zita's mind that it would be very difficult to keep off that particular subject because it would be in the thoughts of them both, whatever else they said in words.

Because she found it hard to refuse him definitely, she said:

"I promise I will ... come if I can, but it ... may be impossible ... I do not know. This morning I was lucky ... and I was able to ... slip away before ... anybody else was ... awake."

"As I did," the King said with a smile. "Give me your hand."

Zita put out her hand towards him, and because the horses were standing still after so much exertion, he pulled off her riding-gloves and lifted her hand to his lips.

She felt the hard pressure of them against her skin, and instinctively, without her meaning to, her fingers tightened on his.

"There are no words, and anyway they are not necessary, to tell you how much I want to see you again," he said softly, "and I shall also add that if you do not come, then I will get in touch with you and we will meet, however many difficulties there may be, or however many people try to prevent it."

There was something in the way he spoke which made Zita feel afraid.

"I am aware that I can get in touch with you at The Golden Cross," he went on, "but I would prefer for you to tell me where else we can meet, or at least where I can write to you without anybody being suspicious."

"There is ... nowhere ... except for ... The Golden Cross," Zita said quickly.

"That is not true," he replied, "but I suppose I must be content with knowing that at least I can find you there."

She did not answer, and the King, who was still holding her hand, lifted it once again to his lips.

"You know as well as I do, Zita, that although you have tried to remind me of my duties as a King, I am still a man and entitled to the feelings and emotions of one."

He kissed the back of her hand again and then he turned it over and his lips were on her palm.

It gave Zita a strange feeling she had never known before.

She felt as if his lips sent a streak of lightning up her arm, into her breast, and then it touched her heart.

It was thrilling and yet there was something spiritual about it which she could not explain.

Because she was shy, and at the same time was alarmed by her own feelings, she took her hand away and as she did so Pegasus moved restlessly so that it was impossible for the King to hold on to her.

She looked at him, her eyes wide and very green in the sunshine.

"Good-bye," she said softly.

"*Au revoir*, Zita," the King answered in French.

For a moment they looked at each other and Zita thought they were saying so much more than could ever have been expressed in mere words.

Then because she knew time was passing she turned Pegasus and set off, knowing that she could approach the Palace from a different direction and there was no likelihood of her encountering the King, who would go in at the front entrance.

She rode very quickly, being determined to put Pegasus into his stable long before the King reached the front door, where the grooms would be waiting for him.

Only when she was in her own bedroom did she realise that it was not yet eight o'clock and the housemaid had therefore not yet called her.

So much had happened and she had passed through so many strange emotions since meeting the King that she was prepared to believe a day, a year, or a century had passed since she had slipped out of the Palace as the stars were still fading.

She took off her riding-clothes and lay down on her bed, but all the time she was thinking of the King and of his suggestion that she should go with him to his Castle in the clouds.

"If I were not who I am," Zita told herself, "it would be a very exciting thing to do."

Then she knew that if she did so, she would become like *La Belle* and all the other women whom *Madame* Goutier had told her had captured the affections of the King for a very short while and whom he discarded apparently quite callously for the next pretty face which attracted him.

Zita wondered if they felt humiliated and unhappy.

Then she was sure that anybody who lost the King after they had been close and intimate with him would feel as if the sun had gone out and they were in darkness.

"It is an outrageous suggestion!" she tried to tell herself.

But she knew, however much she might try to incite herself to anger against him, that if one played with fire one must expect to get burnt.

'I shall never again know such an attractive, fascinating man,' she thought.

Just to be with him made her feel as if her brain was

unusually alert and her whole body was alive with a strange, mysterious excitement.

She wondered if that was the way the other women had felt, knowing that their time with him was short and they could hold him only as long as he found them beautiful and desirable.

She knew that he "made love" to them, although she was not quite certain what that meant, and she wondered what she would have felt if the King had kissed her lips instead of her hand.

When he had kissed her palm it had been like a streak of lightning, half-pleasure, half-pain, shooting through her.

Perhaps, she thought, that was what people meant when they talked of the ecstasy of love.

Quite suddenly she was still.

The word "love" seemed written on her mind in letters of fire.

Could it be possible that what she felt was love? If it was—then what sort of love?

Although the King had suggested that she should go with him to his Castle and he wanted to make love to her, he had not said that he loved her.

Nor—and it now seemed strange—had she thought at the time that that was what he had meant.

Love!

It was a word that had been so often in her dreams, and yet when she had been with the King somehow it had not arisen.

She wanted to see him, to look at him, and it was exciting to listen to him. But because he was a King, she had not thought of him as a man, a man she might love and who would love her.

All the time they had been together, she had enjoyed her subterfuge of deceiving him into thinking she was a waitress from The Inn of the Golden Cross and had been intent on making him curious and parrying his questions with the skill of a duellist who had met somebody worthy of his steel.

Now what had been a fantasy, a game, had suddenly become serious.

The King had asked her to go with him into his own country, to the Castle she had heard about because of the part it had played in the history of Aldross as well as Valdastien.

She had the idea that even her father had never visited it.

"A Castle in the clouds!"

She said the words to herself and thought it would be very exciting to see it and be alone with the King as she had been this morning, when they had sat in the arbour and talked as she would never have been able to talk with him in the Palace.

"But it is all over," Zita told herself, "and it would be a great mistake for us to meet again tomorrow morning."

Then as she thought of how he had extracted a promise from her, she could feel again his lips on the palm of her hand.

She looked down at the hand he had kissed, almost expecting to see the imprint of his lips there.

As she thought of his mouth against her skin, she felt run through her a little echo of the thrill his kiss had evoked.

"Am I in love?"

"Is this love?"

"What is love?"

The questions followed one after another, and because it was impossible to lie in bed because she felt too restless, Zita rose and went to the window to look out at the mountains.

She wondered what it would be like to be alone with the King with the snow-capped peaks above them and the great vista of the country of Valdastien below.

She could hear his voice.

"I want to make love to you!"

*

The day seemed to pass slowly, almost interminably, from the moment her maid came to call her, to the time when she knew that the King would be meeting the Prime Minister and the Statesmen to discuss their national affairs.

By this time she was sure her father and mother would have realised that he had no intention of proposing marriage with Sophie, and so would Sophie herself.

Almost as if by thinking of her sister she conjured her up, Sophie came into the room.

She was wearing one of her new gowns which had been bought especially for the King's visit, and her hair had been arranged in the manner which Zita had suggested and had been snubbed for her pains.

But the expression on Sophie's face was not in keeping with either her gown or the style in which she wore her hair, and she looked, Zita thought, dull, disappointed, and resentful.

"Tell me what is happening, Sophie," she said as her sister crossed the room to sit down opposite her in an armchair.

"Papa is taking the King to a dinner and I have been left behind with Mama."

"That does not sound very exciting," Zita replied. "You do not like politics, Sophie, and that is what they will be talking about."

As she spoke she realised that Sophie was not listening, but after a moment she said, and the words seemed to come from her lips in a rush:

"The King has not spoken to Papa, and he has not proposed to me!"

"I am sorry. Are you very disappointed?" Zita asked sympathetically.

"Not really," Sophie replied. "Mama is very angry and says he had no right to come here raising our hopes, but I find him intimidating and very dull. When he talked to me he always seemed to be thinking about something else."

She looked at her sister and said:

"I shall now ask Mama to invite the Margrave to stay, and I feel quite sure he will wish to pay his addresses to me, which is what I would really like."

"Then I hope he will marry you and you will be very, very happy," Zita said sincerely.

"I do not think that anybody could be happy with the King," Sophie remarked. "Mama says he is not only selfish but has a very bad reputation, and I would not like to be married to a man like that."

"I agree he would make a woman very unhappy," Zita said quietly.

"I must go back to Mama. We are dining together," Sophie said, rising to her feet. "You had better stay up here just in case the King should come back unexpectedly and see you."

"That is unlikely," Zita replied, "but anyway I am quite content to be here with my book."

She spoke lightly, thinking her sister would smile at the idea, but Sophie merely walked from the room, shutting the door behind her.

"So the King has escaped being trapped into matrimony," Zita said beneath her breath.

For the first time it flashed through her mind that if he did not wish to marry Sophie perhaps he would like to marry her.

She had never thought of such a thing in the excitement of meeting the King by her subterfuge in defiance of her mother's instructions.

Then she remembered what he had said about taking a Hungarian wife, and she knew that, although he might wish to have her with him in his Castle in the mountains, he was quite determined that the Hungarian temperament, "impetuous, impulsive, wild, and emotional," as he had described it, was not desirable in his Queen.

'I suppose I am all of those things,' Zita thought ruefully.

She had always found it impossible to be quiet, prosaic, unemotional, and controlled, like her mother.

"The true fact is," she went on to herself, "I have no ambitions to be a Queen. If a King were the man I loved, I would share his life as if we were ordinary people and not as

Rulers over a country, permanently at the beck and call of our subjects."

Zita thought of how her father loved to go off on his own and be free of all the trappings of Monarchy.

That was what the King did in a different way when he went to Paris.

Once Sophie was married to the Margrave, perhaps she would be able to find an unimportant Grand Duke or Prince who would be as impatient of pomp and circumstance as she was.

Then she had the uncomfortable feeling that no man in whom she was interested and who was interested in her would be able to excite her in the same way as the King did.

He looked so majestic, he rode so magnificently, and there were those inescapable vibrations between them and the magical way that they could read each other's thoughts.

"I am not in love! I am not! I am not!" Zita wanted to shout aloud.

But she had the uncomfortable feeling that it was all bravado, and that when she rode away from the King to hurry back to the Palace she had left her heart behind.

*

Zita finished her dinner, which she had eaten alone, waited on by a footman who had difficulty in repressing his yawns after the lateness of last night's Ball.

As he brought in the coffee and set the silver tray down beside her, he said:

"There's a note from His Royal Highness which I regret I forgot to bring up earlier."

Zita looked in surprise at the note and saw it was in her father's hand-writing.

She opened it quickly to read:

I wanted to come upstairs to see you, Dearest, before we left for the dinner, but I have been delayed and it is impossible.

I have decided we will go off on our explorations tomorrow morning, as soon as the King has left.

If we linger, there is every chance of our being prevented from leaving at the last moment, which would be very disappointing.

I suggest therefore you ride to meet me at The Inn of the Golden Cross, accompanied of course by a groom, and wait for me there.

The King will be driving straight on into Valdastien, and when I have changed my clothes we will set off on our "adventure."

I will leave a note for your Mother, and I suggest you do the same.

Bless you, Dearest Child,

Your affectionate father.

Zita stared at what her father had written and read a great deal between the lines.

It was quite obvious that her mother was going to make a great fuss if he proposed to take her away on one of his expeditions as he had said he would.

Therefore, if her mother was not aware of what was happening until after they had left, there would be nothing she could do about it.

It was really very clever of her father, Zita thought, and it was the way she might have planned things herself.

He would drive with the King to The Golden Cross, his valet would have the native costume he always wore on his expeditions ready and waiting for him, and as soon as he had changed they could set off together before anyone had any idea of what was happening.

'Papa is as good an intriguer as I am,' Zita thought.

She wished she would tell him how she had intrigued and confused the King by appearing first as a waitress, then alone on Pegasus, and how, as he had not the slightest idea that she was Royal, he had suggested taking her with him to his Castle in the clouds.

It was a fascinating story, but she knew her father would

be very angry at what he would think was a great impertinence on the King's part.

He would also feel insulted that his daughter should be mistaken for the type of woman who would accept such an invitation when it was offered to her.

"Unfortunately, it is something I shall have to keep from Papa, but I know he would in a way enjoy hearing how clever I have been," Zita told herself.

Now she had a lot to do before she went to bed, and she left the School-Room to get everything ready.

When she had returned to the Palace yesterday she had put her peasant-dress away in a locked drawer in her bedroom.

Now she got it out and found that in her haste to change back into her riding-habit when the King had driven away with her father, she had packed the apron trimmed with lace which Gretel had lent her.

'I must return that,' she thought.

It would be easy to do so, as she would be leaving her riding-habit at The Inn of the Golden Cross for her eventual return to the Capital.

When she was with her father in the mountains she always wore her peasant-dress even when she was on horseback.

This was much easier than to keep changing, and it meant that all she required could be rolled up and attached to her saddle-bag.

These comprised simply a nightgown, two fresh blouses, underclothes, her brushes and combs, and her washing-things.

Now she packed everything she thought she would require, including the ribbons for her hair and several pairs of the long white stockings which reached to her knees.

They were much more comfortable, as were the low shoes with their silver buckles, than the riding-boots she wore with her habit.

Because she felt so free and unrestrained in her peasant-clothes, she thought they were symbolic of her own feelings when she had been with her father in the past.

Imagining they were both incognito, they would go off to meet much more amusing and certainly happier people than they met at the Palace.

Now she told herself that there was no possibility of her taking Pegasus out early in the morning to meet the King.

The horse would have a long day in front of him, and it would be quite enough for him to ride first to The Inn of the Golden Cross and then ride again for many hours.

It would in fact be very much longer than usual, if her father was going, as he had proposed, to the mountain at the far end of the range.

They might perhaps have to stay a night on the way, but Zita was not certain of the exact distance.

She thought perceptively that her father would have chosen it because as he had never been there before, there would be nobody there whom he knew or who knew him.

She could understand how it might be embarrassing for him to meet his "special friends" if he had his daughter with him.

Then she thought that if her father had secrets, so had she, and she would have to be very tactful.

If he wished to flirt with some pretty Inn-Keeper like the ones she remembered in the past, she would certainly make herself scarce and not interfere with his enjoyment.

"It is the only fun poor Papa ever has," she told herself.

Although she supposed it was reprehensible because he was a married man, she could understand how he must find it imperative at times to escape from the boredom of the Palace and a wife who always appeared to be finding fault.

"I wish I could marry a commoner," she said aloud, "a jolly peasant who would laugh and sing his way through life."

Then she knew she was too intelligent to be content with

just an ordinary man, and that when she did get a chance of listening to the Prime Minister and the other Statesmen, she found them very interesting and very enlightening.

As she put the last of her clothes ready for the morning, she knew she would always find any conversation with the King a thrilling experience, which in a way was somehow linked with the thrill and excitement she had felt at the touch of his lips.

Because they were a part of him, and because when she met his eyes she had the same feeling as when she was aware of his vibrations, she knew that being with him was in fact very different from being with any other man.

Perhaps it was something she would never find again. Was it love?

She could not decide whether it was or not, but undoubtedly the question was there.

Because it frightened her, she wanted to run away and never think of it again.

Chapter Six

Riding with her father at the foot of the mountains, Zita thought she should be happier than she had ever been before, but somehow something prevented her from finding this adventure with him as wonderful as it might have been.

Every morning when she woke she felt as if there were a stone in the place where her heart should have been.

Even though they laughed and joked together, and climbing up the sides of new mountains was thrilling, still there was something missing.

At night, alone in the bedroom of the small Inn at which they stayed, she would find, although she tried to prevent it, her thoughts were only of the King.

In not meeting him at five o'clock the next morning as he had expected, she wondered if she had been unnecessarily cruel.

Had he waited and waited, hoping she would come?

Then she told herself with a metaphorical shrug of her shoulders that of course he had neither waited nor minded.

Why should he worry about one woman, when he had dozens of every sort, shape, and size yearning for him, longing for him, and ready to fall into his arms?

She told herself that his only interest in her had been that she was unpredictable and his failure to find an explanation for either her looks or her intelligence had irritated him.

She was sure she was not mistaken in thinking that because he prided himself on his intuition he expected to sum up any woman he met quickly, and was seldom proved wrong or disappointed.

'Perhaps he has been disappointed in me, and that will be very good for him,' Zita thought.

At the same time, she knew that the one who had been hurt in this unequal contest was herself.

She was intelligent enough to reason it out that it was because she had met so few attractive men that the King had seemed overwhelming and doubtless more fascinating than he really was.

"If I had ever been in Paris, as he has, or even in England, I should very likely have found a dozen men no less attractive than he. At least I should not have felt that he was something so unusual and unique that it is difficult to forget him," she told herself.

Actually she found it impossible, and although during the day she forced herself to concentrate on her father, she was aware that just behind everything she was saying, the King was always there, like a skeleton at the feast.

At the same time, it was a delight to ride without restriction and to know that when evening came she did not have to face her mother in either a fault-finding or a sulky mood.

To begin with, things had not gone entirely according to plan.

The King had been late in leaving the Palace, and Zita, waiting for the carriages to arrive at The Inn of the Golden Cross, could not help worrying if they were late because he had lingered for longer than he should have done, waiting for her.

Then she told herself that she was making herself out to be far more important than she really was.

Yet doubtless it had irritated him that she had not obeyed his orders, and it might be annoying him still more that now he would never learn the secret of an unpredictable waitress.

Then she told herself firmly:

"As soon as he has left Aldross he will never think of me again."

At the same time, because there was the chance that the

King would either write to her or make enquiries at the Inn, she was forced to take Gretel into her confidence.

"You've seen His Majesty again?" Gretel exclaimed. "How exciting! What did he say to you?"

"It was just by chance," Zita replied truthfully, "that we met out riding."

"Has he proposed to Princess Sophie?" Gretel enquired.

Zita shook her head.

"I bet that's your fault!"

Zita laughed.

"I think the truth is that the King has no wish to marry anybody. After all, he has been a bachelor for a long time."

"That's true," Gretel agreed, "and the travellers who come through here have lots to say about the actresses and such-like whom he entertains at the Palace. But I shouldn't be saying that to you."

"Why not?" Zita asked. "I have heard about them anyway."

Gretel looked surprised, but she went on:

"It's been a thrill for us to see the King in the flesh, but if he's not going to marry Princess Sophie, I expect it's the last time he'll come to Aldross."

"Why should you say that?" Zita asked in some surprise.

"Because he's too busy elsewhere when he goes away from Valdastien."

"In Paris!"

"And who'll blame him?" Gretel asked. "In France they understands what a man likes in the way of amusement! What have we to offer except folk-dancing and too many snowy mountains?"

Zita laughed, but at the same time she was thinking that it was the truth, and that small countries like Valdastien and Aldross could be very dull for an adventurous man.

When, nearly an hour late, the King arrived with her father, he changed carriages and went on into his own country without entering the Inn.

As she watched from an upstairs window Zita felt that as

he was not even curious enough to ask if she was still there, their acquaintance, if that was what it had been, had definitely come to an end.

Her father had come bustling up to the room which the King had used on his arrival.

"Sorry to be late, my dearest," he said. "Maximilian was late for breakfast and the Prime Minister also insisted on seeing him for a last word."

He flung his plumed hat down on the bed as he said:

"God knows why Statesmen always have something extra to say, rather like people who invariably add a postscript to their letters."

Zita laughed.

"The truth is, Papa," she said, "they are not as quick-brained as you or I, and therefore all the important things they ought to have said in the first place come to them later when they are in bed or in their baths."

Her father laughed as she intended him to do.

Then she went to talk to Gretel in the next room while he changed.

They left their clothes behind at The Inn of the Golden Cross, and having accepted a glass of wine from the Proprietor, they set off, excited at what lay before them.

"We certainly shall not reach the place I was planning to stay tonight," the Grand Duke said, "but we will stop half-way and look at the lake where you first bathed and learnt to swim."

"I would love that!" Zita exclaimed. "And I recall that the Inn was very attractive."

It was more comfortable than she remembered, and the food was so delicious that they stayed there for three nights.

They climbed high up the mountains and Zita swam each day in the lake that was the same as it had been ten years before, unspoilt by the encroachment of tourists.

Sometimes torrents in the winter would alter the scene on the sides of mountains that she and her father had visited and loved, but the little lake was mirror-still and pale blue from the sky above it, and the rocky pine-covered crags descended sheer to the water.

It was so lovely that Zita felt it might have been part of a fairy-tale.

She found herself wondering as she swam what she would feel if the man she loved was swimming with her. After they had bathed they would sit in the sunshine and talk together of their dreams, and of course . . . their love.

Then she tried to convince herself that she had everything she wanted in being with her father.

Moreover, it was very unlikely she would ever find a man of her own rank who would not be horrified at the idea of his wife swimming in a public place, even though there was nobody to see her except himself.

"I am very, very lucky that Papa is so unconventional," Zita told herself severely, "and how can I be so ungrateful as to want anybody else but him?"

She was very affectionate and attentive to her father and she knew she made him happy and that he was enjoying himself.

"This is the first holiday I have had for a long time," he said.

"That is what it feels like," Zita teased, "but I know you disappeared for nearly a week last year, and Mama was so disagreeable that all the servants in the Palace talked of giving notice!"

"I remember now," the Grand Duke said, "but it still feels a very long time since I have been so free."

"We will make the very most of it," Zita promised.

The next day they set off fairly early and lunched in a little chalet where climbers slept when they were scaling that particular mountain, and which also provided rough but palatable food for occasional travellers.

There were two men there who were just about to attempt to scale the peak of the mountain above them.

Her father talked to them and they respectfully accepted his advice on how they should attempt it, although Zita was almost certain they did not recognise him.

Then while the sun was still very hot they set off again, and now the Grand Duke was able to point out a mountain that seemed taller than the rest, where the snows from the winter not only covered the peak but were deep in the crags quite far down on the barren rocks.

"It looks very high, Papa!"

"It is," the Grand Duke agreed. "Maximilian told me that it is higher than any other mountain in Valdastien."

"Has the King climbed it himself?" Zita asked.

"He may have," the Grand Duke replied indifferently, "since he told me that the Inn at which we shall be staying is quite comfortable."

Instantly, because the King had spoken of it, Zita wondered if he had been there incognito, perhaps with some attractive woman he fancied.

Then she thought that since the King had a penchant for actresses, it was unlikely they would appreciate what could be the considerable discomforts of country life and country Inns.

She could imagine them scented and bejewelled, enjoying the luxury of thick carpets, elegantly furnished bedrooms, and being waited on and cosseted by an inordinate number of servants.

If they had known privation and discomfort before they were successful, that would certainly not be an attraction now.

For her it was the reverse. She loved the bare wooden boards in the Inns in which they stayed, with perhaps just a rug or two made from a bear-skin or that of a goat.

It was fun to sleep in the box-beds that the peasants preferred because they could draw the curtains close in the cold winter nights, on a mattress made of goose-feathers, and being obliged to wash in cold water was certainly no hardship in the summer.

"Why are you silent, my dearest?" the Grand Duke asked unexpectedly. "I am missing your laughter."

"Actually I was thinking how lucky I am to be with you," Zita replied, "and to enjoy the simple life where we wait on ourselves, with nobody to fuss whether we do or do not look exactly as we should."

The Grand Duke laughed.

"I am sure your mother would think it very reprehensible that I prefer a silk scarf round my neck to a tie, and that if it is hot I ride in my shirt-sleeves."

"At the moment I am concerned not with my appearance but my stomach," Zita replied. "I am hungry and I am hoping that our dinner when we arrive this evening will be a substantial one."

She remembered that their luncheon had been mostly of goat's-milk cheese, and the Grand Duke replied:

"If Maximilian is to be believed, the food is excellent, so I hope we will not be disappointed."

Once again the King's name gave Zita a strange feeling in her breast, but she told herself it was nothing more than she had felt ever since she had met him at The Inn of the Golden Cross.

Too, she had had a very strange feeling when she saw him drive away until there was just a cloud of dust in the distance and then an empty, even if beautiful, view over the valley.

"That is the end of the story," she had said to herself.

She felt that a chapter in her life had closed and there would be no mention of the King in those that followed.

An hour later, the sun was sinking lower in the sky and it was not as hot as it had been, when finally they left the valley to start climbing up the side of a mountain.

There was a twisting, winding path through the pine trees and they climbed higher and higher until Zita began to feel they must have lost the way.

The horses could manage only a slow pace uphill, when just above them appeared an attractive chalet with gabled windows which looked as if it might have been an illustration in a picture-book.

"We have found it, Papa!" Zita exclaimed. "And it is very attractive."

There were tables and chairs outside the Inn, and to her surprise several travellers were seated at them, drinking glasses of wine.

This was usual at most of the mountain Inns at this time of the year. At the same time, because this particular one was so isolated, Zita had somehow anticipated that they would be the only guests.

They took their horses to the back of the Inn where they found there were stables which were somewhat primitive but adequate.

There appeared to be nobody in charge of them, and Zita took Pegasus into a stall where there was plenty of hay and water, which showed that the stables were regularly in use.

She unsaddled him, took off his bridle, and patted him affectionately before she shut him in and went to find that her father had already dealt very effectively with his own horse.

They walked from the stables to the Inn, which was a very short distance, and instead of going round to the front her father led the way to the kitchen door.

As he opened it he knocked on a wooden panel, saying in a loud voice,

"Is there anybody here to welcome a weary traveller?"

There was the sound of a woman's voice calling out for somebody, and then from a passage which led to the front of the building, a woman appeared.

The moment Zita saw her she felt she must have seen her somewhere before. Then, as she came towards them, smiling a welcome, she looked at the Grand Duke and gave a cry that seemed to echo down the narrow passage.

"No, no! It can't be true!"

"Névi!" the Grand Duke exclaimed, and held out both his hands to her.

It was then that Zita remembered that Névi had been the lovely woman who had been so delighted to see her father many years ago when they had been travelling together in another part of the country.

She could remember him saying,

"I always keep my promises, Névi, and this time I have brought my daughter to meet the prettiest woman in the whole of Aldross!"

She recalled now how comfortable Névi had made them, and although she was older she still looked very lovely and her eyes were sparkling as she looked up at the Grand Duke to say:

"I can't believe it! I've thought of you so often, but I was sure you'd never come here!"

"Once I returned to the place where you used to be," the Grand Duke said, "but you had flown."

"It was Rudolph," Névi said in a low voice. "He was so wildly jealous that he insisted that we move to a part of the country where he thought you'd never find me."

"I tried," the Grand Duke said simply.

Then he added in a different voice:

"Perhaps it will be embarrassing for you if my daughter and I stay here."

"Rudolph was killed in a climbing accident a year ago," Névi replied, "and now I own the whole place and run it with the help of several nice girls and one of my nephews who's learning the business."

She gave the Grand Duke a flashing smile before she added:

"By the blessing of God, we have no-one staying with us at the moment, so not only are my best rooms free, but I can look after you and the gracious *Fraulein* as I'd wish to do."

As if while speaking she suddenly remembered Zita's existence, she turned towards her and exclaimed:

"But you've grown! You're no longer the little girl I remember."

"We all grow older," the Grand Duke said, "which unfortunately is something we cannot prevent."

He spoke in his joking manner, but Zita heard an irrepressible note of youthful excitement in his voice that had not been there before!

As she looked at her father, she thought that he not only looked extremely handsome as he always did, but also younger than she had seen him for some time.

There was a large, comfortable room for him overlooking the front of the Inn, and another which Zita sensed Névi did not consider quite so grand but which had a view over the valley.

"I hope you'll be comfortable," Névi said as she showed Zita into it, "and please ask for anything you require. I can't tell you how happy it has made me to see you and your honourable father again."

Zita was quite certain that Névi knew who her father was but was prepared to please him by pretending that she had no idea of his true identity and rank.

When they had washed and Zita had arranged the ribbons in her hair, which she did not wear when she was riding, she went downstairs to find that a table for dinner was laid for them in the garden outside the chalet.

It was partly enclosed by shrubs and made Zita think of the arbour where she had sat with the King and surprised and confused him by the things she had said to him.

It flashed through her mind that she had been very foolish not to see him once again as he had asked her to do.

Yet it would have been almost impossible for her to take another horse from the stables, which she might have difficulty in saddling, rather than Pegasus.

She thought of the King now travelling, as she was sure he would be, towards Bosnia.

Perhaps there he would find the Princess he required as a wife. Then all she would ever hear of him would be the gossip that percolated inevitably from his country to Aldross.

But if he did not find a wife at Bosnia he could go to Serbia, and, as she had pointed out to him, there were many other small Principalities attached to them.

In all of them there would undoubtedly be women who would find him extremely attractive and would be only too willing either to marry him or to let him make love to them.

"What am I keeping myself for?" Zita asked herself, as she saw her father watching Névi as she came towards them carrying their food with an expression in his eyes that was very revealing.

'She attracts him,' Zita thought, 'just as he attracts her, and what could be more natural than that they should be happy with each other, and why should it be wrong?"

As they enjoyed their dinner, which was delicious, and drank the local wine, which was like sunshine, Zita heard her father speak in a voice that was deeper and different from the way he had ever spoken before.

She felt perceptively the excitement growing within him, which intensified every time Névi brought the coffee and sat beside Zita's father.

"Now tell me," she said, "everything you've done since we last met. "I've missed you, I can't tell you how terribly I have missed you."

"You are even more beautiful than you were when I last saw you," the Grand Duke replied.

Zita drank her coffee, then without saying anything she moved away from the table to leave them talking to each other.

She knew it would be tactless for her to stay, for she wanted her father to enjoy himself and she thought that tonight she must not listen for the soft laugh she had heard before coming from his room when she had awakened in the moonlight.

She walked away from the Inn, moving under the pine trees along one of the little paths beaten down through the years by people following it up and down the mountain.

The sun was sinking in a blaze of crimson glory and the first stars had not yet appeared in the sky.

There was the scent of pine from the trees, and Zita felt almost as if she were part of the woods and that the life that pulsed within her was theirs also, and they both drew it from the same source.

She walked on for a little way, still following the path where it twisted behind the Inn, and she came to where there had been a fall of rocks that had left the side of the cliff bare.

It had carried the trees away with it, so she had a view of the valley and the evening mist coming up from the meadowland and rising mystically to make everything look as if it were part of a dream.

She stood thinking that such beauty could never be portrayed on canvass even by the greatest artist.

It could only be held in the memory. One would not only remember the loveliness of it but like a secret shrine it would always be there to raise the heart and soul.

Because it was so perfect, she found herself wishing with an intensity that she could not suppress that she could share it.

She felt that there was only one person who would understand and see it as she was seeing it, although why she should think that about him she had no idea.

'We never had time to discuss beauty,' she thought.

She wondered why she had been so stupid as to quarrel with him and take him to task instead of sharing with him the feelings which she sensed would be the same as hers.

"I have been a fool!" Zita told herself.

Then, because the beauty of what she was seeing was somehow intolerable, she turned to return to the Inn.

As she did so, she was aware that somebody was approaching.

She could hear footsteps, then was aware of a man moving between the trunks of the trees, catching only a glimpse as he passed behind first one, then another.

She resented the intrusion.

She thought swiftly that it would be a bore if she had to stop and talk as was customary in that part of the world.

She was conscious only of the beauty of the valley and the pain within her breast because she could not share it with the King.

Then as she stood hesitating, wondering whether if she turned her back the stranger would pass by and not stop to chatter, he emerged from between the trees and she thought for a moment he was just part of her imagination.

Then when he came nearer she saw incredibly, unbelievably, that it really was the King!

For a moment she felt as if she were turned to stone, then as he came towards her with a smile on his lips she forgot everything except that he was there.

She could never afterwards remember if he spoke or if, as she thought, he held out his arms.

She knew only that impulsively, eagerly, and without thought, she reacted to the feelings that already possessed her and did as her heart told her.

As she ran to him his arms went round her, then his lips came down on hers.

All she was conscious of was that the sunset was part of him, the light of it blinding, and his kiss was what she had wanted, longed for, and dreamt of, although she had not been aware of it.

Now the lightning which had moved to her heart when he had kissed the palm of her hand was streaking through her whole body, moving from her breast up into her throat and to her lips.

Then as the King held her closer and his lips became more possessive, more passionate, she felt as if he carried her into the sun itself, and the heat of it seemed to burn its way through her body, and yet it was part of her soul.

Only when she felt it was impossible to feel such sensations and not die of the wonder of them did the King raise his head.

"My darling!" he said, in a voice which was strange and very unsteady. "I thought I should never find you!"

Then, before she could speak, he was kissing her again, kissing her fiercely, demandingly, possessively, as if his fear of losing her made him want to make her his forever.

Only when time had stood still and a century might have passed in the King's arms did Zita give an inarticulate little murmur and hide her face against his neck.

Her heart was pounding and she felt as if every nerve of her body was throbbing with a rapture that was indescribable.

She was alive, more pulsatingly alive than she had ever been in her whole life, and she could only think that this was love as she had never expected it to be.

"My precious!" the King said. "How could you go away in that damnable way? I have been frantic, desperate, in case I could never find you again."

"I . . . could not . . . help it," Zita managed to whisper.

"When I learnt at The Golden Cross that they had no idea where you were," the King said, "I thought I would go mad!"

"You . . . asked for me?" Zita enquired.

"I sent somebody to do so," the King replied, "just as I have sent a dozen of my most trusted servants to make enquiries in the City as to where you were or where I could find you."

Zita stiffened and he said:

"It is all right, my precious. They were very discreet, but how could I have thought you would be here?"

"B-but . . . why are you . . . here?"

"I was looking for you."

As he saw the surprise in her eyes, he said:

"I will explain in a moment, but now all I want to do is to kiss you!"

He did not wait for a reply but found her lips and was kissing her until she could think of nothing except that her whole body seemed to burst into flames and burn with a sensation that was so thrilling, so ecstatic, that it was impossible to think but only to feel.

Then as the King kissed her and went on kissing her, there was a sound behind them and Zita heard her father's voice:

"Zita! What the devil do you think you are doing?"

It was difficult for the moment to come back from the rapture that possessed her, which had carried her into the sky, to the realisation that she was in the King's arms and her father was looking at her incredulously, as if he could hardly believe what he saw.

Then as she strove to find her voice, the King turned his head and the Grand Duke exclaimed:

"Your Majesty!"

As if he could hardly believe what he was seeing, he added:

"I had no idea that you knew Zita!"

The King stiffened and turned towards the Grand Duke, taking one arm from round Zita while the other still encircled her.

For a moment the two men looked at each other. Then the King asked harshly:

"Is Zita yours, Sire? It is something which had never crossed my mind."

"Mine? Of course she is mine!" the Grand Duke answered sharply. "But as I had no idea Your Majesty had even met her, I find this completely astonishing."

He walked nearer to them and as he did so Zita glanced up at the King and realised what he was thinking.

For a moment it did not seem possible!

Then, because she was afraid he might say something which would reveal to her father the very strange story of how they had met and the King's ignorance of her identity, she said quickly:

"Forgive me . . . Papa for not . . . telling you, but I met . . .

His Majesty . . . one morning when we were both out . .
riding."

As she spoke to her father the King set her free, and now
he was looking not at the Grand Duke but at her, and the
surprise on his face would have been ludicrous had she not
been nervous of what he might reveal.

In a voice which sounded very unlike his own, the King
said:

"Am I to understand, Sire, that Zita is your—daughter?"

"Of course she is my daughter!" the Grand Duke said
testily, as if the King was challenging him.

"I did not—meet her when I was—staying with you," the
King persisted.

The Grand Duke looked slightly embarrassed.

"My wife thought it best if you met only Sophie, and Zita
therefore remained in the background."

Then, suddenly realising that there was no reason for
him to be on the defensive and that that should be the
King's role, he said:

"I would, however, Your Majesty, like an explanation as
to why your very short acquaintance with my daughter, for
it can be nothing more, should entitle you to behave as you
were . . . "

Before he could say any more, the King interrupted:

"I would be most grateful, Sire, if you would give your
permission for Zita and me to be married as soon as possible."

His voice was firm and there was none of the astonishment or suspicion that had been in it before.

It was now the Grand Duke's turn to be surprised, and he
stared at the King as if he could hardly believe what he had
heard.

Then as he comprehended the King's request and was in
fact extremely gratified by it, he said:

"This is certainly something I did not expect, Your
Majesty, and I think we should talk about it over a glass of
wine."

It was then that Zita came back to reality.

As if waking from the dream she had been dreaming ever since the King had kissed her and carried her into a world so wonderful, so rapturous that she could hardly believe it, let alone understand it, she was aware that these two men were deciding her future.

It was almost as if she stood aside and saw the years ahead being planned for her without her having any say in the matter.

She knew that while her whole body vibrated and pulsated for the King, and the fire that he had awakened within her was still burning, her mind told her something very different.

The King and her father were smiling at each other with an understanding as if there was little need for words because they were so in tune with each other.

But she felt a cold, icy wind pass through her as if the snows on the mountain above were touching her and putting out the heat of the fire.

She looked at her father and saw how pleased he was by the King's request. Then she looked at the King and while her body would have moved more closely to him, her brain said: "No!"

She could see, almost as if she had been shown them, the women who had loved him, who had been part of his life, whom she had heard about and imagined.

Women who, like *La Belle*, were doubtless waiting for him at this moment.

She saw them moving into his life and out of it, being replaced by others and still others, and she knew this was something she could not endure and live with.

It all flashed through her mind in the passing of a second, and as her father was just about to take her arm and lead her back to the Inn, she said, and her voice was clear and sounded surprisingly calm:

"Before you go any further, I have something to say in this matter. While of course I am deeply honoured at the suggestion of His Majesty that he should marry me, my answer is: 'No! I will never be his wife!'"

She did not wait to see the astonishment on the King's face or her father's.

She ran straight past them, and following the path that led through the trees, she ran faster and still faster until she reached the Inn.

She sped up the stairs, and finding her own room threw herself down on the bed and hid her face in the pillow.

She knew she was shutting herself out of Paradise.

At the same time, an instinct for self-preservation, which was stronger even than the rapture and wonder of love, told her that only in this way could she survive.

*

A long time later Zita heard her father come upstairs and go into his bedroom.

He did not come to say good-night to her, and she thought he was doubtless angry that she had behaved as she had. He would also be ashamed because she had insulted the King.

"It should not be an insult to refuse to marry a man," she argued with herself.

However, she was quite sure that the King would feel not only insulted but humiliated that the first time he had asked a woman to marry him she had refused.

Then she told herself that she should be the one to be insulted.

After all, he had offered her a very different position in his life, and if he had been so lacking in perception as to think she would accept such a proposition, then it was his own fault that in consequence she now had no wish to be his wife.

But arguments, however logical, did not assuage a feeling of consternation or expel the uneasy conviction that her father could bring pressure to bear on her to change her mind.

'The King's behaviour will ruin our holiday,' she thought resentfully.

Then she knew that he had ruined it already because she could never again feel happy or free.

He had kissed her and the rapture of it was still with her, so that even to think of him was to feel a thrill running through her, and her lips were still soft from the pressure of his.

"I love him . . . I love . . . him!" she admitted to herself.

But she knew that where he was concerned, love was not enough.

Perhaps they would be happy together for a short time, until he became bored with her as he had been with other women.

He would slip away to Paris, or like her father find amusements locally, to relieve the monotony of a marriage which was always the same, year in and year out.

"How could I bear it?" Zita asked herself.

She thought that when that happened, however much she tried to control her temper and her emotions, she would want to kill the woman who had supplanted her in her husband's affections—and indeed might actually do so.

She imagined what it would feel like to be alone in the Palace or in a great State-Bedroom and know that the King was in the *Château,* having gone down the secret passage after the Court had retired to bed, to enjoy the excitement of a new face, a new allurement which had an attraction his wife could no longer give him.

'Then I would really die . . . or else commit some . . . terrible crime for which nobody would ever . . . forgive me,' Zita thought despairingly.

And yet the King's lips had awakened sensations in her that she had no idea existed, and she was aware that if she lost him now, she would never find the same rapture with any other man.

As she thought of him she heard very soft footsteps on the uncarpeted passage, then a door opened and closed, and she knew who had gone to her father's room.

She was aware then that it was not only the King's infidelities that kept her from marrying him but also her father's.

"All men are like that!"

She could almost hear somebody saying the words aloud to her, and the warning remained in her mind.

Men were like that, and she accepted it.

But what she would not accept was the agony, the humiliation, and the frustration of being the unwanted wife of a husband she adored but who no longer had any use for her.

'I am different from Mama, for I could never forgive or forget,' she thought, 'and it would be impossible for me to sit tamely waiting for my husband's return.'

She thought then that perhaps she would be goaded into causing a scandal by taking a lover and flaunting him.

But she had the uneasy feeling that if she loved the King as much as she did now, there would never be another man she could allow to touch her or come close to her in any way.

The agony that she would endure in the future was so vivid in her mind that she knew that anything she suffered now would sink into insignificance compared to what she would suffer later.

"I will not marry him . . . I will . . . not!" Zita told herself.

And yet she knew that already her body was aching for him, and she had the frightening feeling that if he suddenly appeared she would want to throw herself into his arms as she had done when he came to her from between the trees.

"I love him, I love him!" she cried in her heart.

But there could be no solution and no happy ending, and all she could do was to compel her father to understand that she had made up her mind and nothing he could say could change it.

Through the open window with the curtains undrawn

she could see the stars, and because they seemed to hurt her and somehow made the pain she was suffering more intense, she got out of bed and shut them out.

She felt with only the candlelight in the pretty but austere bedroom it was easier to think calmly and quietly.

Her bed was not the box type she had slept in the previous nights. Instead, the wooden back was carved by a local craftsman with a design of flowers and fruit, and the base with various birds.

The carving was painted in the traditional way of the hill craftsmen, and the mattress was of goose-feathers, very soft and comfortable. But Zita felt as if she were lying on stones, each one piercing her and making her feel that she was a martyr.

"Which I am, to love," she murmured bitterly.

She got into bed again and decided that because it would be impossible to sleep, she would not blow out the candles.

She knew that in the darkness, she would yearn, dream, and cry for the King.

But it was impossible not to think of him, and she now wondered where he could have gone.

He was not staying at the Inn, for Névi had said definitely that they were the only guests.

"Why should I worry about him?" she asked herself defiantly. "The sooner he accepts what I have said, the better."

She was sure *La Belle* or somebody like her would be only too willing to console him, but to think of the beautiful dancer waiting at the *Château* made Zita feel as if she had thrust a dagger into her heart.

But she was determined that she would not weaken.

"I will not marry him . . . even if he begs me on his knees," she said proudly.

Even as her voice was little louder than a whisper and might have been that of a ghost in the small room, the door opened.

Zita gave a gasp of surprise—it was the King!

Chapter Seven

THE King shut the door behind him and walked slowly towards the bed.

He had changed into a long dark robe that nearly touched the ground and he had a silk scarf round his neck.

He looked strange, and the robe made him seem taller and in a way more impressive than he did ordinarily.

Zita stared at him wide-eyed until she found her voice:

"W-why are you . . . here? You have . . . no right . . . to come into . . . my room."

"I have to talk to you, Zita," the King said quietly, "and as you might run away, as you have done before, there is no other way I can be certain you will listen to me."

"I do not want to listen to you. We have . . . nothing to say to each . . . other."

"On the contrary, I have a great deal to say, and frankly you have no alternative but to hear me."

"It will do no good," Zita said. "I have made up my mind . . . and . . . nothing will . . . change it."

As she spoke she realised that the King, who was standing beside the bed, was looking down at her and that at the same time in her surprise at seeing him she had raised herself straight up against the pillows.

In the candlelight her thin nightgown trimmed with lace was very revealing.

Quickly and defensively she pulled the sheet up higher, and she thought the King's lips twisted in a smile before he sat down on the mattress and faced her.

The mere fact that he was near to her made her heart beat frantically, and she could feel the vibrations from him so strongly that it was hard to think of anything else. But she said aggressively:

"You have no . . . right to be here. You know it is extremely . . . unconventional, and Papa would be very . . . angry if he knew of . . . it."

As she spoke she thought that her father would find it hard to complain when he himself was behaving in an even more reprehensible manner.

But because the King agitated her she found it impossible to look at him, and she waited for his reply, feeling helplessly that whatever she said, he would pay no attention.

"Ever since we have known each other, Zita," the King said after a moment, "you have been unconventional, and now it is my turn."

"That was . . . different."

"In what way?"

"When I pretended to be a . . . waitress at The Inn of the Golden Cross, I only wished to . . . look at you, because Mama had said I was to keep out of sight while you were at the Palace."

"Your behaviour was hardly what I might have expected from the Grand Duke's daughter."

"All I wanted to do was to see you close to . . . and know if all the gossip I had . . . heard about you was . . . true."

"So you were curious about me?"

"Like everybody else in Aldross."

"I can only hope that I lived up to their expectations," the King said sarcastically. "But when I saw you, Zita, something happened to me which has never happened before."

Because she could not help herself, Zita glanced quickly at him and thought irrepressibly that he looked very handsome in the candlelight.

There was also an expression in his eyes which made her remember the way he had kissed her and the ecstasy she had felt as if he were carrying her over the peaks of the mountains and up into the sky.

It had been more wonderful than anything she had ever dreamt of or imagined.

Then, because she knew he was waiting, she found herself asking in a rather small voice:

"What did . . . happen?"

"I fell in love!"

"That . . . is not . . . true!"

"It is true, and now I am going to tell you a story. I think because we are so closely attuned and can read each other's thoughts, you will understand what I am trying to say."

Zita told herself she should not listen, she should order him to leave her bedroom, but before the words could leave her lips the King said:

"My mother was Hungarian."

Whatever Zita had expected him to say, it was not this, and her eyes widened as she said:

"Hungarian? I had no idea!"

"Very few people know of it, simply because my mother is very seldom mentioned even in Valdastien. The reason is that her marriage to my father was a morganatic one."

Because she was so surprised, Zita dropped her hands, which were holding the sheet against her breasts, to stare at him in astonishment.

"Morganatic?" she questioned.

"My father fell in love with my mother as soon as he saw her, and although she was of noble birth, she was not Royal. So they were married secretly in Hungary."

The King paused before he continued:

"When they returned to Valdastien and to my grandfather, there was nothing he could do but accept that the marriage was valid."

"It must have been very . . . romantic," Zita said beneath her breath.

"It was," the King agreed, "but my mother was not only beautiful, she was very Hungarian."

He smiled as he said:

" 'Impetuous, impulsive, wild, and emotional'!"

He paused before he said very quietly:

"All the things my father found irresistible and which I find irresistible in you."

"But you said . . ." Zita began.

"I know what I said," the King interrupted, "and that is something I have to explain to you."

He looked away from her as if he was delving back into the past.

"When my mother died I was six at the time, and my father was so distraught, so utterly desolate without her, that he did not care what happened in a future which did not contain the woman he loved, So he allowed himself to be pressured into a marriage which was politically advantageous for Valdastien."

His eyes came back to Zita as he said:

"I think you, of all people, are aware what an arranged marriage can mean to a man who knows what love is, and finds that without it his marriage is empty and meaningless."

Zita knew he was speaking of her father, but she did not say anything and the King went on:

"The moment my Step-mother came to the Palace she was determined to erase the memories of my mother from everybody's mind as if she had never existed. She was helped in this by the Statesmen who had always been somewhat ashamed that my father's wife was not the Queen, but only allowed the title of 'Her Serene Highness.' "

The King's voice sharpened as he said:

"Every portrait of my mother was either destroyed or stored away where nobody could see it. She was never mentioned and I was not allowed to talk about her."

Zita made a little murmur of horror and the King went on:

"I adored my mother. She was the most beautiful, warm, loving person in the whole of my small life, and like my father I felt as if the world had come to an end and I was lonely in a way that I cannot describe to you."

Zita had the vision of a small boy lost in a large Palace with people round him who were suddenly hostile to everything that had mattered to him.

She made an impulsive little gesture as if to put out her hand, then checked herself because she was afraid that if she touched him she would no longer be able to maintain her resolve not to marry him.

"It was not only that I was not allowed to talk about my mother," the King went on, "but the Nurses she had chosen for me were changed, and everybody round me spent their time in instilling into my mind that everything that was Hungarian about me must be suppressed and erased from my character."

The way the King spoke told Zita how terrifying it had been and how much he had suffered.

"I was punished if I spoke a word in Hungarian," he went on. "If I cried I was punished for being uncontrolled and over-dramatic. My Tutors were instructed by the Queen that the most important lesson I was to learn was that of self-control. By that she meant that I was never to show my emotions."

"How could anybody have been so unfeeling or so cruel to a child?" Zita cried.

"The answer to that is quite simple," the King said with a twist of his lips. "The Queen was jealous. She had fallen in love with my father after she married him, but she knew that never in a million years would he love her, and his thoughts were always with the wife he had lost."

"I suppose that was . . . hard on her . . . too," Zita murmured, thinking of her mother.

"Very hard, but that is often the case where arranged marriages are concerned," the King said, "and that is why I was determined I would never be forced into one."

"And yet . . . I thought that you came to Aldross . . .

thinking that you might ... marry Papa's ... daughter," Zita said hesitatingly.

"My Prime Minister told me that I must marry to save the succession, since if I died without an heir there was every likelihood that Germany, having established their Federation, might interfere in the affairs of Valdastien."

"That is what we were afraid of," Zita said, "and therefore, because it would be politically advantageous for both countries, Papa believed you would offer for Sophie."

"I suppose I might have done so," the King said gravely, "though I would certainly have looked round the other nations first. But then I met you."

"Are you really ... saying that ... changed your ... mind?"

"When I turned from the mirror," the King replied, "the sun was on your hair and for one incredible moment I thought my mother had come back!"

"Am I ... like her?"

"That is another thing I have to tell you," the King said. "I had often heard stories of your grandmother and how beautiful she was, and how very, very Hungarian in temperament!"

His eyes twinkled before he went on:

"So before I came to Aldross, thinking it would interest your father, I looked up her Family-tree and found there was one rather obscure branch of the Esterhazys who had married into the Frazcozskis, who were my mother's family."

He paused before he said with a smile which made Zita feel as if her heart turned over in her breast:

"So you see, my darling, we are actually related to each other."

"But ... you said you had no ... wish to ... marry an ... Hungarian!" Zita protested.

"It had been so drummed into me," the King replied, "that the Hungarians were everything that was wrong from a Monarch's point of view, that I had almost begun to believe it! So at that moment I was fighting against my love for you."

Zita looked surprised but she did not speak and he continued:

"I was on the defensive, telling myself that although I desired you, the only place you could hold in my life was a transitory one, because the fires that were consuming me would burn themselves out as they had done in the past."

"That is . . . what I have . . . heard," Zita murmured, "and that is . . . why I will not . . . marry you."

"I knew that was the reason," the King remarked.

Again she looked surprised, and he said:

"Have you forgotten that I can read your thoughts as you can read mine? I knew, my precious, when you ran away this evening saying that you would not marry me, that you were afraid of the future and of the way you thought I might make you suffer."

Now Zita stared at him in astonishment.

"How . . . could you have . . . known that?"

The King made a gesture with his hands.

"How can I explain what I feel for you?" he asked. "I can only say that I love you as I have never loved any woman in the whole of my life!"

"How can you be . . . sure?"

"I am sure, because you are everything I have ever wanted and thought I should never find."

His voice seemed to challenge her as he said:

"Of course there have been women in my life, and once I was free of the severity and restrictions of my Step-mother, I enjoyed my freedom as I think most men would have done."

"You went to . . . Paris!"

"Yes, Paris," the King replied, "and I found there most of the joys that I had missed living in the dull, depressing gloom of the Palace in Valdastien."

"I can . . . imagine what . . . those . . . were."

"Of course," the King went on. "There were women to tell me I was attractive, women to make me laugh, women with whom I could dance, and women who were only too eager to do anything I wanted as long as I gave them jewels, gowns, and parties which had to be more extravagant and more outrageous than any that had taken place previously."

"It must have been . . . fun!"

"I certainly enjoyed it," the King said frankly, "but after a while I began to find that, like too much *pâté de foie gras,* it began to satiate me."

He smiled ruefully before he continued:

"When my father died and I inherited, I came back almost thankfully to Valdastien, to my horses, my mountain-climbing, and the other sports I had always enjoyed when my Step-mother did not prevent me from taking part in them."

"What happened to . . . her?"

"She was German and I sent her home."

"German?"

"She came from the Duchy of Mildensburg," the King explained. "The people there are partly Prussian, which I think you will agree accounts for a great deal of what I suffered under her jurisdiction."

"And she was . . . prepared to leave . . . Valdastien?"

"She had no choice!" the King said in a hard voice.

Zita knew then that he had compelled his Step-mother to go, and she gave a little sigh as he went on:

"Then I was my own master and could do what I wanted."

"And that meant . . . bringing women to the . . . *Château.*"

"How do you know about that?"

"I think everybody in Aldross knows why the *Château* . . . adjoins the . . . Palace."

The King looked at her for a long moment before he said:

"So that is another reason why you are refusing to marry me!"

Because he was so perceptive, Zita felt the colour come into her cheeks, and she was unable to look at him.

"Shall I tell you," he said in a low voice, "that it is now empty, and that is how it will remain."

"Until you . . . need it . . . again?"

"*If* I need it again," the King said, "it will be because you have either died or no longer love me."

"How can I be . . . sure of . . . that?"

"By using your instinct," he answered. "I think we are both aware that our instinct is something very Hungarian, which would be impossible to explain to other people, but which is so much a part of us that we cannot discount or ignore it."

"I . . . I still think it would be a . . . mistake to marry you," Zita said. "I understand what you are . . . trying to tell me . . . of course I understand . . . but I really have . . . no wish to be a Queen . . . and . . . "

She was hesitating, trying to find the right words, and the King said:

"You are just trying to make out a case against me, and I do not intend to listen. I am going to marry you, Zita, either with or without your consent, and I have no intention of allowing you to say: 'No!' "

Because he spoke in a low, calm voice, it took Zita a moment to realise how determined he was.

Then she felt she was confronting a will of steel and she knew that he was prepared to fight her. She also had the uncomfortable feeling that he would eventually be the victor.

But she was still uncertain, still afraid of her own love for him, which seemed to invade her whole body so insistently that it was more a pain than a pleasure, and she was frightened by it.

"If you go away now," she said quickly, "not only out of this room, but out of my life, we shall both . . . forget each other. You will find a suitable Queen who will not mind when you have other . . . interests, and if you think about it sensibly, since we are both Hungarian our marriage could never be anything but tempestuous . . . and we might eventually . . . tear each other to . . . pieces."

She was thinking as she spoke how violently jealous she would be of him.

Then it flashed through her mind that if he behaved as she expected, she might try to kill not only the woman who had supplanted her in his affections but him too.

The King was watching her eyes and to her surprise he gave a little laugh.

"Oh, my darling," he said, "do you think I do not know what you are thinking? Because for one incredible moment I thought that the Grand Duke was your lover and not your father, I felt the same. I wanted to commit cold-blooded murder so that I could take you from him. You are mine, Zita, and I will kill any man who touches you."

The way he spoke was so violent that Zita stared.

"We may quarrel," the King went on, "but however much we may rage at each other, it will be no more than a passing thunderstorm. When we make it up there will be sunshine, and love will carry us again into the heart of the sun, burning with the fire of it."

There was a note of passion in his voice that seemed to vibrate through Zita.

She felt as if the fire of which he spoke flickered within her and there were little flames rising in her body as there had been when he had kissed her.

"I love you," the King said, "and because I will allow nothing in the world to make me lose you again and suffer as I have these last few days, I am giving you a choice between two alternatives. And you have to choose now!"

"What . . . are they?"

"The first is that you give me your word of honour that you will marry me," the King answered. "And because it is important, as you agreed, that I should try to set up a Federation amongst the other countries which I intend to visit, I shall take you with me and we will be married in exactly two weeks."

"That is . . . impossible!"

"The alternative," the King went on as if she had not spoken, "is that I will stay here now and make you mine. You will belong to me, and when I tell your father in the morning what has happened, I think he will agree that you must allow me to put a wedding-ring on your finger."

"You are blackmailing me!" Zita cried angrily. "How dare you!"

"I am doing so because I know I can make you very happy," the King replied, "as I know you will make me. I know too that we both have things to do in the world which could be of inestimable benefit to other people, starting with my country and with yours."

"That sounds very glib," Zita retorted, "but you know as well as I do that you are really giving me no chance of . . . refusing you."

"Of course I am giving you no chance," the King answered, "simply because, my darling, while I have said that I love you, there is no need for you to tell me you love me, for I know it."

His voice was very beguiling as he went on:

"I knew it when you quivered to my kiss on the palm of your hand, and I was very, very certain of it when I kissed you just now, and we both felt as if we had reached the gates of Paradise."

Because this was so palpably true, Zita found it difficult to know what to say.

Then as the King waited she felt she must make one last stand rather than surrender herself without striking a blow in her own defence.

Her chin went up as she said:

"You did not ask me to . . . marry you until you knew I was . . . Papa's daughter!"

The King smiled.

"I wondered when you would remember that, and so I have a question now to ask you. Why do you think I spent two hours climbing down the mountain from my Castle to this Inn, knowing I would find your father here tonight?"

"I have no idea."

"For the last three days after you did not meet me as I had begged you to do," the King said, "my most trusted men were scouring your City to find you, but always returned to tell me they had failed."

"That was because they were looking in the wrong places," Zita remarked.

"Your friends at The Inn of the Golden Cross kept your secret well," the King went on, "and there was therefore only one thing I could do."

"What was that?"

"Ask the help of the Grand Duke."

"Why should you think he would help you?"

"Because," the King replied, "I had decided, since I knew you belonged to me, I must marry you morganatically, and as you were a citizen of Aldross, the one person who could make our marriage acceptable to Valdastien would be the Ruler of your country."

"You intended to . . . marry me . . . morganatically?"

"I knew it was the only way I could be happy for the rest of my life," the King said simply.

"I . . . I can . . . hardly believe . . . it!"

"I will make you believe it," he replied, "but I do not pretend, my darling, that it will not make things very much easier for both of us that you can reign with me as Queen. There will certainly be no opposition from my Prime Minister, and my subjects will love you."

"I was not thinking about them . . . when I said I would not . . . marry you."

The King read her thoughts and knew that *La Belle* and the other women whom Zita had in her mind stood between them.

"I know exactly of whom you were thinking," he said quickly, "but you have to forget them. They were just flowers by the wayside which faded very quickly and were not important because all the time, although I was not really aware of it, I was looking, searching, and yearning for you."

He gave a sigh as he said:

"How could I have been so stupid as not to realise that the Hungarian part of me could only be satisfied with a Hungarian, and now that I have found you, I will be a complete person, and so will you, my precious love."

He bent forward as he spoke and put his arms round Zita.

Somewhere at the back of her mind she thought she should resist him, but it was too late.

His lips were on hers, and as he touched her she felt her whole being surrender itself to him, and as her head fell back against the pillow the King bent over her.

Their vibrations linked one with the other and his lips drew her heart from her body, and she was no longer herself but part of him.

He kissed her and once again the earth was left behind and they were part of the stars shining overhead.

He kissed her until she was pulsating and burning with the wonder of it, and she felt flames of fire rising in her breasts, and knew that the King was burning too.

He raised his head and she could only stare at him and murmur incoherently in a voice that did not seem like her own:

"I . . . love . . . you . . . I . . . love . . . you!"

"Say that again!" the King commanded. "Say it until you make me believe it!"

"I . . . love . . . you!"

"When will you marry me?"

She made a little murmur that was half a sob as she said:

"Tomorrow . . . tonight . . . even if you only . . . love me for a . . . short time . . . it will be . . . worth it!"

"I shall love you forever! And you know, my lovely one,

there are no words in which either of us can express the height, the depth, and the wonder of our love."

Because she knew that was true, Zita put her arms round his neck.

"I love you until . . . it is impossible to . . . think of anything else except that I am desperately . . . afraid of boring you . . . and you will leave me. If you do . . . I will want . . . to die!"

"I shall never leave you, and you will never leave me," the King said. "I know, my darling, that anyway we will have to live at least a thousand years to convince each other of our love, which we have known in many other lives. We have been so very, very fortunate to find each other again in this."

Zita pressed herself a little closer to him.

"If that is true," she said, "then we will never lose each other, and you are right . . . we will be together for eternity because we are not . . . two people . . . but one."

The King did not answer.

He only kissed her until the stars fell from the sky and covered them.

*

The cheers of the crowd were deafening as the Royal Carriage with the bride and bridegroom came from the Palace into the main street of the Capital, which was packed with people.

Everywhere there were flowers; flags flew on the top of every building and from every window, while the people were waving their hats and their handkerchiefs.

Zita, holding on tightly to the King with one hand, waved with the other and blossoms were thrown into the open carriage as they moved slowly behind the Troop of Cavalry which was escorting them to the border.

Only when they were out of the main part of the City and

into the open country where the crowd was less dense did the King ask:

"You are not tired, my darling?"

"How could I be tired," Zita replied, "when I kept thinking how grateful I was to have found you, and that I was not having to marry somebody like that incredibly boring Margrave of Baden-Baden?"

The King laughed.

"I think he is very well suited to your sister."

"That is what she thinks too."

"And I am very well suited to you," the King said, "except that I do not believe your mother approves of me."

"Actually, Mama thinks we are very well suited as she never approved of me either!" Zita replied, and they both laughed.

A shower of rose-petals prevented them from speaking until they had passed a crowd of School-children.

Then the King said:

"I wanted to tell you how beautiful you looked in your wedding-gown, and you are just as beautiful now in your smart bonnet with its green feathers."

"Mama said that green is unlucky, but it is very lucky for me," Zita said, "as are the emeralds you have given me."

She looked down as she spoke at the huge emerald she wore together with her wedding-ring.

"It is the colour of your eyes," the King said softly, "and because your eyes glint with a strange fire when I excite you, that is what I will see tonight."

The way he spoke made Zita blush before she asked:

"You have not . . . told me where we are . . . staying for our . . . honeymoon, but I think I can . . . guess."

"Then you have cheated and read my thoughts," the King said, "but where else could we go except to my Castle in the clouds?"

"That is where I was sure you would take me," Zita said, "although I was . . . afraid you might be . . . ashamed to do so."

"I am not in the least ashamed," the King replied. "I want to take you there because—and this is the truth, Zita—I have never been there with another woman. I always loved it because it was my mother's favourite Palace, which she decorated in a way that is typically Hungarian."

"Then I shall love it as you do," Zita promised softly.

The King took her hand and raised it to his lips, which evoked an even louder cheer from the crowd who saw it and who thought it was a very touching gesture which they would always remember.

At The Inn of the Golden Cross they were to change carriages from the one that belonged to her father to one that belonged to the King.

But Zita was surprised to see that instead of an open Victoria there was waiting for them a very smart Phaeton, drawn by four horses and built so lightly and with such large wheels that she knew it would be very swift.

There was no chance of her expressing her surprise until they had said good-bye to the Courtiers who had accompanied them from the Palace, and Zita had a special word for Gretel.

"It is all due to you, Gretel, that I am so happy," she said quietly so that nobody else could hear, "and I have brought you a special present which I hope you will wear and remember us both."

"I could never forget you anyway, Your Majesty," Gretel replied.

Zita knew as she walked away that Gretel would be thrilled with the very pretty brooch she had given to her, and which had the King's and her initials set in diamonds on an enamel background.

Then the King himself was driving her away in the Phaeton, escorted only by four out-riders who kept very much in the background.

"How could you think of anything so exciting?" Zita asked when the Inn was out of sight and she no longer had to wave to those who were left behind.

"I am in a hurry," the King said simply, "and the State Carriage and the Cavalry would have taken double the time that we shall take in reaching the Castle."

"I have never seen such an unusual Phaeton before."

"It comes from Paris," the King explained, and his eyes were twinkling.

"As long as that is the only thing you import from Paris into Valdastien," Zita remarked, "I will not complain!"

"I am quite certain you will want to go to Paris and buy new gowns there," the King answered. "But there is no hurry, and for the moment I find you exquisite and very, very desirable in those which come from your own country."

"I think you are really disparaging the dressmakers of Aldross!" Zita retorted. "I promise you that each gown I bought, and there was no time for many, is labelled as being a French Model."

She gave a little laugh as she added:

"In fact, as Mama disapproved of most of them, they are, as you can imagine, very *chic!*"

"I will give you my opinion of them later," the King said. "But I am sure that nothing could be more alluring than the nightgown you were wearing when I proposed to you in your bedroom at the Inn!"

"Proposed!" Zita exclaimed indignantly. "You merely informed me that I *had* to marry you! In fact, I am just a captive in chains, bound behind the victor's chariot!"

"I think if the truth be known," the King replied, "I am the captive! I lost my freedom, which was very precious to me, the first moment I set eyes on you."

"Are you already regretting it?"

"I will answer that question a little later," he answered, and whipped up his horses to make them go faster.

The Castle was more impressive and more beautiful than Zita had anticipated.

Built high up on the snow-peaked mountains, it was a dream Palace and she knew as the King lifted her up into his arms and carried her over the threshold into the huge Hall that he was the King of her dreams just as she was the Queen of his.

There was a gypsy orchestra playing in the Salon, where there was wine for them to drink a toast with the heads of the staff.

Then they were free to go up the stairs hand in hand.

The King showed Zita first the State-Rooms with windows overlooking the most amazing view she had ever seen in her life.

Then he took her farther along the wide corridor, which was decorated with paintings and furniture that she knew were outstanding, to their Suite of rooms.

As he showed Zita into the first one, which was the "Queen's Room," she knew it was the loveliest bedroom she had ever seen.

She thought that only somebody who thought like an Hungarian and was Hungarian could have designed anything so beautiful.

The sight of it instantly raised her heart in a way she found difficult to explain, except that she was aware that the King felt the same.

"This was my mother's room," he said softly.

"I feel she knows we are here together," Zita answered, "and is very . . . very glad that you are . . . happy."

To her surprise, the King did not kiss her but walked back to shut the door and lock it.

Then he came back to Zita and undid the ribbons of her bonnet to throw it down on the sofa.

"All the servants here are of Hungarian origin," he said, "and I gave orders that they were not to intrude or worry us unless we rang for them."

The way he spoke made Zita looked at him enquiringly, then he was undoing the buttons of the light coat she had worn for travelling and threw that down on the sofa as he had her bonnet.

Then he put his arms round her and said:

"You have been my wife for nearly three hours, and I have not had a chance to kiss you."

As Zita lifted her lips to his he added:

"I think, my precious, after such a morning ceremony, a Wedding-Breakfast, and quite a long drive, you should rest."

The way he spoke made the colour rise in Zita's cheeks and he laughed gently and said:

"That is a conventional word which for the moment means something very different."

Then slowly, as if he was deliberately not hurrying, the King drew his finger along the side of her cheek until it touched the point of her chin.

It gave Zita a strange feeling and she thought his touch was like a little flame that seemed to run through her and make it hard for her to breathe.

"You are so beautiful!" he said. "I find it hard to believe that at last you are really mine and that you will not fly out the window and disappear, or that I shall not wake up and find I am merely dreaming."

"We are in a dream-world, my darling husband, and we must never . . . step out of . . . it."

"I think it would be impossible to do so," the King said, "and to make sure we can go on dreaming, I want to tell you how much I love you and how much you mean to me."

As he spoke his lips sought hers, but it was only a very tender kiss and a very quick one.

Then gently, so that she could hardly believe it was happening, the King unbuttoned her gown and it slipped from her shoulders to the floor.

A moment later he lifted her onto the bed, and as she lay there sinking into the softness of it, her eyes dazzled by the evening sun that enveloped the valley and a sky that seemed as translucent as the snowy peaks of the mountains, she was not alone.

The King was close to her and she could feel the hardness

of his body against the softness of hers as he pulled her closer and still closer.

She made a little murmur of sheer happiness, then he was kissing her hair, her eyes, her small straight nose, and lastly her lips.

"I love you . . . oh, wonderful, marvellous . . . Maximilian . . . I love you!"

She was not certain if she said the words or if they were singing in her mind.

Then the fire which had been burning in them all day carried them, with the rapture of love, up over the peaks of ecstasy into the sky.

Zita felt that the King had taken not only her heart and made it his but also her soul and . . . her body.

They were one, not only for this life but for those which stretched over the horizons of eternity into the infinity of the Paradise of Love.

ABOUT THE AUTHOR

BARBARA CARTLAND is the bestselling authoress in the world, according to the *Guinness Book of World Records*. She has sold over 350 million books and has beaten the world record for five years running, last year with 24 and the previous year with 24, 20, and 23.

She is also an historian, playwright, lecturer, political speaker and television personality, and has now written over 350 books.

She has also had many historical works published and has written four autobiographies as well as the biographies of her mother and that of her brother, Ronald Cartland, who was the first Member of Parliament to be killed in World War II. This book has a preface by Sir Winston Churchill and has just been republished with an introduction by Sir Arthur Bryant.

Love at the Helm, a novel written with the help and inspiration of the late Earl Mountbatten of Burma, Uncle of His Royal Highness Prince Philip, is being sold for the Mountbatten Memorial Trust.

In 1978, Miss Cartland sang an Album of Love Songs with the Royal Philharmonic Orchestra.

She is unique in that she was #1 and #2 in the Dalton List of Bestsellers, and one week had four books in the top twenty.

In private life Barbara Cartland, who is a Dame of the Order of St. John of Jerusalem, Chairman of the St. John Council in Hertfordshire and Deputy President of the St. John Ambulance Brigade, has also fought for better conditions and salaries for midwives and nurses.

As President of the Royal College of Midwives (Hertfordshire Branch) she has been invested with the first badge of Office ever given in Great Britain, which was subscribed to by the midwives themselves.

Barbara Cartland is deeply interested in vitamin therapy and is President of the British National Association for Health. Her book, *The Magic of Honey*, has sold throughout the world and is translated into many languages.

Her designs, *Decorating With Love,* are being sold all over the USA and the National Home Fashions League made her "Woman of Achievement" in 1981.

Seventy-five newspapers in the United States and several countries in Europe carry strip cartoons of Barbara Cartland's novels, and *Barbara Cartland Romances* (book of cartoons) has just been published.